An exuberant and magical story of an Armenian woman, Nancy Kricorian's first novel follows its lively heroine from childhood in the old world to grandmotherhood in 1980s America. In radiant, poetic prose, ZABELLE recounts the tale of a spirited woman whose ordinary life is infused with the ghosts and memories of her extraordinary past.

Beginning in a suburb of Boston with the quiet death of Zabelle Chahasbanian, an elderly widow, the narrative shifts back in time to her childhood in the waning days of Ottoman Turkey, where she barely survives the 1915 Armenian Genocide and near starvation in the Syrian desert. Zabelle's journey encompasses years in an Istanbul orphanage, a fortuitous adoption by a rich Armenian family, and an arranged marriage to an Armenian grocer, who brings his unseen bride to America. Through each of the often comic interactions and battles that she wages in her new country—with a domineering mother-in-law, a tradition-bound husband, Americanized children, and the man she secretly loves—images and shadows from a long-lost world accompany her.

"Kricorian brings a poet's grace and a keen sensitivity to voice this Armenian experience… Literature is richer for her efforts."
—Rick Moody, author of *The Ice Storm*

Zabelle

NANCY KRICORIAN

AN AVON BOOK

AVON BOOKS, INC.
1350 Avenue of the Americas
New York, New York 10019

The Grove/Atlantic, Inc. edition contained the following Library of Congress Cataloging
in Publication Data:
Kricorian, Nancy.
  Zabelle / Nancy Kricorian.
    p.   cm.
  1. Armenian American women—Massachusetts—Boston—Fiction.
I. Title
PS3561.R52Z23   1998
813'.54—dc21   97-36237

First Bard Printing: March 1999

BARD TRADEMARK REG. U.S. PAT. OFF. AND IN OTHER COUNTRIES, MARCA REGISTRADA, HECHO
EN U.S.A.

Printed in the U.S.A.

OPM 10 9 8 7 6 5 4 3 2

To the memory of

Mariam Kodjababian Kricorian

Three apples fell from heaven: one to me, one to the storyteller, and one to the reader of this tale.

Zabelle

Heaven and Hell

It was Zabelle Chahasbanian's seventy-fifth or seventy-sixth birthday. No one knew for sure because Zabelle's birth date had been lost with her family when she was a child. As she gingerly descended the stairs to the church function room, Zabelle assumed she was on time for a meeting of the Ladies Aid Society.

When a roomful of her family and friends shouted, "Surprise," Zabelle felt a hand twist her heart. She sat heavily in a chair, fumbling in her purse for her nitroglycerin pills. While the tablet dissolved under her tongue, Zabelle closed her eyes. The hand released slowly. Exhaling deeply, Zabelle gazed at the blurred faces hovering around her. As their features came into focus, the names floated just beyond reach. Finally the faces and names realigned themselves, but the damage had been done. In that moment, Zabelle had started to come unmoored from her present life. She was on a boat whose anchor had worked itself loose, and the tide was pulling it slowly away from shore.

Zabelle lived in the upstairs apartment of a two-family house in Watertown, Massachusetts. She had raised three children there. Decades before, her eldest son, Moses, had fled the nest, eventually settling in the distant land of California. Her son Jack had strayed only as far as the downstairs apartment, which he now inhabited with his wife and two college-age daughters. Zabelle's daughter, Joy, had never married and lived with her mother still.

A few days after the birthday party, Joy opened the pickle crock on the back porch and discovered her mother's stockings soaking in the brine. Next she found her mother's pocketbook in the bread box and a stick of butter in the medicine cabinet. When Joy questioned her mother, the old woman groped for words, as though sorting through lentils for rocks. Then she trailed off midsentence.

Joy was afraid. Every morning of her forty-eight years, she had taken breakfast with her mother. She faced the prospect of life after Zabelle the way a blind man might face news of a distant tidal wave. But the fear passed, and life seemed to return to normal.

One afternoon a few weeks later, Zabelle's granddaughter Elizabeth sat on the porch with her grandmother while the old woman hemmed the girl's new skirt. Elizabeth, with her legs folded under her, rested her head on the back of the couch and stared out through the grapevine that was unfurling its first green leaves.

"Why am I doing this, Joy? I taught you to sew," Zabelle said without lifting her eyes from the work in her lap.

"Grandma, I'm Elizabeth."

Zabelle shook her head. "Sorry, honey. My mind is wandering." She patted the girl's hand and asked, "You want ice cream?"

"I don't eat ice cream."

"Some yogurt, maybe?" Zabelle disliked seeing the collar bones poking out of her granddaughter's shirt.

"Stop it. I'm not hungry."

Zabelle shook her head. "In Hadjin, everyone wanted a plump hen for a wife. You look like the last scrawny chicken someone would think to throw in a pot."

Elizabeth groaned, "Grandma."

"I'll be back," the old woman said. She shuffled inside. When she returned a few minutes later, she said, "Open your hand."

Zabelle placed an antique silver thimble in her granddaughter's palm. It was from the old country.

"Grandma, I can't take this." Elizabeth examined the thimble, which was decorated with coiling silver tendrils.

"I want you to have it," insisted Zabelle.

"I can't sew."

"Doesn't matter." Zabelle closed her hand over Elizabeth's, the thimble like a seed in the girl's palm.

As her hold on this world slackened, Zabelle turned her sights on the next. She spent long hours reading her Bible, lingering over the descriptions of heaven in Revelations. *The city was pure gold, like unto clear glass. . . . The foundations of the wall of the city were garnished with all matter of precious stone.*

God would give her a new body, one without pains in the hands or the droop and sag of old age. There would be no dust in heaven, no frayed patches on the Oriental rugs. No one would be sick or hungry. She wouldn't be plagued by nightmares.

When she slept, Zabelle dreamed about the skin-and-bones children in her missionary magazines. They were shades of black and brown, teeth and eyes an awful yellow. Their sticklike arms reached up to her. She placed a grain of rice in each palm, but they clamored for more. In the morning, Zabelle wrote out checks for five and ten dollars to the missionary societies whose publications she read. But the nighttime visitations continued, and soon ancient fears crept out to prowl Zabelle's room.

* * *

Arsinee Manoogian, Zabelle's best friend, began to notice that something strange was going on. The two women talked to each other on the phone every day, morning and afternoon. One morning Arsinee's phone was silent at the appointed hour.

After ten minutes had passed, Arsinee impatiently dialed her friend's number. She let the phone ring ten times and was just about to hang up when Zabelle answered.

"Hello?"

Arsinee shouted, "Are you trying to give me a stroke? Why didn't you call?"

"Arsinee? Is that you?" asked Zabelle.

"Who do you think it is? Billy Graham?"

"I forgot," Zabelle said simply.

"You'll end up like *Digin* Lucia, who has to be reminded to use the toilet."

Several days later, Arsinee muttered under her breath as she dialed, "She'd leave her teeth in the glass if I didn't tell her to put them in her head."

"Who is it?" asked Zabelle.

"Lawrence Welk."

Zabelle dropped her voice to a whisper. "They're coming."

"Who?" questioned Arsinee.

"The Turks," Zabelle said. "They're going to break down the door."

"In Watertown, we have French, Greeks, Italians, and Irish, Zabelle, but no Turks."

"We'll be killed."

"Zabelle, stop this foolishness. Do you want Joy to shut you up in the Ararat Nursing Home?"

"No," said Zabelle.

"Then forget about the Turks."

"I hear voices at night."

"Tell them to pipe down."

"Remember the mother who threw her baby in the river and jumped in after?"

"*Vay babum.* You're going to make yourself crazy with this kind of talk."

At night, long shadows and disembodied voices, speaking Armenian and Turkish, circled Zabelle's bed. She heard fragments of long-forgotten songs. The faces of her mother, father, brother, grandparents, aunts, and uncles came swimming up at her like fish surfacing from the bottom of a pond.

When she woke with her heart thrashing in its cage, Zabelle calmed herself by imagining the life she would lead in heaven. Flowers lined the gleaming promenades. Pastel aluminum siding covered the houses, and fruit hung heavy in the trees. She saw Jesus surrounded by young people in flowing robes, sitting in the shade of a beech tree with silver leaves.

He gestured to her to come closer. "Zabelle," Jesus said, "in my Father's house there are many mansions. What color do you want?"

"Blue," she responded. "With a pear tree, and mint in the garden." She added, "No squirrels."

"We'll see what we can do," Jesus said.

* * *

Jack shut the family market for a few minutes so he could drive his mother to Arsinee's. She was no longer able to walk the distance.

"Don't drive so fast," Zabelle said.

Jack sped up.

"Toros, slow down," Zabelle insisted.

Toros, Jack thought as he glanced at himself in the rearview mirror. He did look like his father. It was as if the old man were slowly taking over from the inside. He pulled up in front of Arsinee's house.

"Joy will pick you up later. Okay?"

Zabelle snapped her purse shut. "Okay."

"You want some coffee?" Arsinee asked as Zabelle entered the front door.

"*Cheh.* It upsets my stomach."

"Come sit down."

Zabelle crossed the Oriental rug and settled into a doily-strewn armchair, next to an end table bearing framed photographs of Arsinee's children and grandchildren. It could have been Zabelle's apartment, even down to the potted philodendron vine growing along the mantel.

"I saw Moses Charles on TV," commented Arsinee.

Moses Charles, the California evangelist, was Zabelle's eldest son, whom she hadn't seen in the flesh for eight years. It still rankled Zabelle that her son had changed his name.

"Waiting on the Lord?" Zabelle asked. This was her son's weekly Bible show.

"No. He was a guest on the 700 Club."

"He visits everyone but his mother," Zabelle said.

"At least he has the excuse of living on the other side of the country. Henry hasn't been here in a month, and he lives ten minutes away."

"You have Dahlia," Zabelle reminded her.

"And your grandson remembers you. How is Peter?" Arsinee asked.

"He's learning Armenian in college. He called to practice new words."

"Any good?"

"Terrible accent, but he tries."

They fell into silence.

"I'm having trouble at night again," Zabelle said.

"Indigestion?" asked Arsinee

"The desert," said Zabelle.

Arsinee, who had been there with Zabelle, knew what the word meant. Arsinee studied Zabelle's face, judging whether to joke or bluster. Tears were sliding over Zabelle's cheeks. Arsinee sighed and took her friend's hand.

On Friday Joy arrived home from work, slipped into a housecoat, and lay down on her bed. She imagined what it would be like to be married to her boss. This time his wife was killed by a hit-and-run driver, and after comforting him in his grief, Joy accepted his offer of marriage. Suddenly it occurred to Joy that she hadn't seen her mother.

She called out, "Ma!" She searched the rooms of the house and the porch. She went to the back gate, she looked in the front yard, and then she knocked on the door to the downstairs apartment.

Joy's niece Elizabeth came to the screen. Joy, who always wore a hat and gloves for a trip to the local mall, stood on the back porch in a housecoat and slippers.

"What's the matter?" asked Elizabeth.

"Have you seen Grandma?" Joy nervously tapped her fingers on her cheek.

"Not since this morning," said Elizabeth.

"I'm worried. You take Lincoln, and I'll go down Walnut. . . ."

Zabelle, meanwhile, crouched on her suitcase in the walk-in closet in the attic. She had been there for most of the afternoon. The lightbulb was burned out and the air musty, but Zabelle felt safe surrounded by her first set of dishes, stacks of Moses's books, Jack's army footlocker, and her husband's dusty suits. After a while the attic's tiny noises grew louder, so she began to softly sing old hymns. But what had driven her to the attic in the first place?

In the midafternoon, Zabelle had turned on the television to find Arlene Francis wiping a tabletop. Arlene Francis, born Arline Kazanjian, was an actress Zabelle admired. Here she was selling Zabelle's favorite brand of lemon furniture polish.

As she dusted, Arlene came closer until her face filled the screen. Zabelle saw perspiration on the woman's upper lip, lines in her forehead, even the pores on her nose. The actress looked directly at Zabelle and whispered in Armenian, "They're coming to get you."

Zabelle flew out of the chair and switched off the television. She hustled to her bedroom, pulled a suitcase from under her bed, and began packing some clothes. She emptied her top dresser drawer of her prized possessions. Into a pillowcase she dropped a battered tin cup, a wooden hand mirror, a set of tortoiseshell combs, a blue paste brooch, and a faded envelope with a Worcester postmark. Zabelle searched the back of the drawer before she remembered she had given the thimble to her granddaughter.

In the kitchen, she threw some food into her suitcase. After dragging her bags to the attic, she found a place to hide.

"She's got to be somewhere in the house," said Elizabeth as she and Joy came in the back gate.

"In the basement?"

"Or the attic. You go down."

Elizabeth took the stairs two at a time. She heard muffled singing coming from the closet near the bathroom.

"There is going to be a meeting in the air, in the sweet, sweet by and by . . ."

"Grandma?"

The song stopped, and there was no response. As Elizabeth walked toward the door, a floorboard squeaked under the thin carpet. She grasped the doorknob, turned it, and met resistance.

"Elizabeth!" Joy called up the stairs.

"Up here." Elizabeth pulled hard. The door gave way. There was Zabelle, sitting on a suitcase in the dark closet.

"Grandma!"

Joy, huffing after the flight of stairs, pushed Elizabeth aside. "Ma! What are you doing?"

"Hiding," Zabelle said calmly.

"From what?" her daughter asked.

Zabelle remembered Arsinee's warning about the Ararat Nursing Home. "Nothing much." She picked up her bags and stepped out of the closet. She handed Joy the suitcase. "You know that blue dress?"

"The blue-and-green flowered one?" Joy asked.

"That's the dress I want to be buried in," Zabelle said. She handed Elizabeth the pillowcase. "This is for you, honey."

"What for?" the girl asked.

Zabelle didn't answer.

* * *

Less than a week later, as the ambulance careened toward Mount Auburn Hospital, Zabelle lay on a stretcher and Joy clasped her mother's hand. Zabelle's eyes were clouded with pain. She could barely talk. Joy leaned close to hear what her mother whispered.

"I came back with the water, and she was gone."

Joy said softly, "Ma, don't talk."

"Toros. And Moses."

"He'll be on the next plane from California, Ma."

"Heaven."

Joy murmured, "Don't leave me."

Joy stopped by the Mardirosian Funeral Home the next day to order a casket lined with blue silk. When she arrived home, she closed the door to her mother's bedroom, as though it were a time capsule. She set up the ironing board in the kitchen and pressed every tablecloth and napkin in the house.

Moses Charles, his wife, and his two sons arrived in Watertown a few hours before the wake. Moses would deliver the eulogy and asked his brother and sister to help him write it. Zabelle's three grown children sat at the dining-room table. The daughters-in-law busied themselves in the kitchen.

Moses tapped his pen on the table impatiently. "So, what was special about Ma?"

Jack and Joy were silent. Jack imagined he was being

quizzed by a hostile schoolteacher. Joy felt as if she were in a rubber dinghy floating in a shark-infested sea.

"There must be something." Moses felt unappreciated. As Jesus said, a prophet had no honor in his own country.

Jack tried, "She . . . uh . . ." Then he froze.

Joy offered, "She made the best stuffed grape leaves. Everyone at church said so."

Moses rolled his eyes.

The four grandchildren watched TV in the living room. Elizabeth grabbed a peppermint candy from the bowl on the coffee table. The taste was from a hundred years ago. It reminded her of a song her grandmother used to sing in Armenian about a cat who got into the butter dish. Elizabeth couldn't remember the words.

Before the funeral, Elizabeth and her sister helped Joy with the baskets, casseroles, and pans of food that people from the church had delivered. Joy found her mother's spare teeth in the dairy compartment and laughed raggedly.

When the phone rang, Elizabeth picked it up. "Hello?"

"Zabelle?"

Elizabeth recognized the voice. "Auntie Arsinee, this is Elizabeth."

"Zabelle?" Arsinee was confused.

"Zabelle's dead, Auntie. You were at the wake last night."

"Elizabeth?"

"Yes."

Arsinee said, "You sound just like Zabelle."

"No, I don't!" yelled Elizabeth. She slammed down the phone and burst into tears.

This was the end and the beginning of Zabelle's tale.

CHAPTER ONE

The Tin Cup

(RAS AL-AIN, 1916)

I remember what it was to be a child—you see the world in pieces. It was like a kaleidoscope, and every time you looked, the colors fell together in a different way, making another pattern. What I know now makes one kind of sense, but what I knew then made another picture.

The day I was born, my father wrote my name and the date in the family Bible, as was the custom. We lived in a house at the top of a hill, and my grandparents shared a walled yard with us where we had a garden. It was my job to pick mint from a bed that grew along the stone wall. After I gave the leaves to my mother, my fingers smelled of crushed mint all afternoon. We had a kitten that I named Moug, because she was gray like a mouse and had a small pink nose. The kitten sat in the lowest branch of the apricot tree, watching me and my cousins play hand games in the shade. The name of our town was Hadjin.

My grandmother taught me how to sew when I was very small, and together we made a doll out of my father's old shirt. The doll had black yarn hair, black buttons for eyes, and a tiny scarlet mouth my grandmother embroidered with satin thread, and her name was Zaza. My mother made a dress for me and one for Zaza from the same cloth.

I was too small to go to school with my cousins, but my father showed me how to write my name. The letters were like insects walking across the paper. Above my name I drew a picture of me, and Zaza, and Moug, and our apricot tree. The apricots were soft like the baby Krikor's cheeks. His hair was very light, almost blond. He sat in my mother's lap, clapping his hands while I danced.

In the afternoon, when Krikor and I lay down to rest, my grandmother told me stories from the Bible, about Noah and the Ark, Jonah and the whale, Queen Esther and how she saved her people. How Lot's wife was turned to salt. How Jesus fed the multitude with the loaves and fishes. She also told about *devs* and *djinns,* some who were evil and some full of mischief.

My cousin Shushan and I got the idea one day to give the baby a bath in the big earthenware pickle jar in the yard. We had taken off the baby's clothes and were ready to put his feet in the brine when my grandmother came out into the yard, shaking the broom, yelling at us. *Khent ek?* Are you crazy? What kind of *djinns* are you girls? She grabbed Krikor and started chasing us around the yard, the baby in one arm and the broom in the other hand. The baby peed all over her dress, and my cousin and I could hardly run because she looked so funny. My grandmother caught up, and the four of us tumbled in a pile, laughing.

One day my father put some clothes in a sack and left the house. My mother was crying into her apron and rocking back and forth in the chair. Grandmother was pulling on her cheeks, because my uncle had departed with my father, so both her sons were gone. I asked, "Where are they going?" No one heard me.

Not very long after that, the rest of the family made bundles and got ready to leave our house. My mother was kneading her hands like dough as she made piles of things to take and things not to take. She kept moving objects from one side to another, and back again. Would two pots be enough? The bedding was too bulky for us each to have one, but how many could sleep on one *doshag?* Should she bring my father's winter coat?

We loaded down the donkey and filled the wagon with sacks of rice, flour, bulgur, and dried fruit. Some clothes, a few blankets. My mother cried about leaving the rugs and the wooden chest she had brought with her from her mother's home. In the chest were the wedding towels she had embroidered as a girl and the needle-lace doilies she had worked. Each knotted loop in the lace was the size of a mustard seed. Strung together, they formed flowers, the sun, and stars.

My grandfather tied a tin cup to a string and made a necklace of it for me. Moug we had to leave behind, and the Bible stayed in its place on the shelf. I took Zaza with me, but somewhere along the road she was lost. Maybe some other little girl picked her up, I thought. She couldn't be lying in the mud under the wheels and feet.

We followed the ones ahead of us and were followed by those behind us, all the Armenians walking together. We abandoned our wagon when we reached the mountains. We climbed hills and mountains, descended into steep valleys, and went up again. It was cold at night; sometimes it poured down rain, and we sat holding a blanket over our heads. The donkey died, so we took what we could carry. To keep us moving, Turkish soldiers yelled from horseback and beat stragglers with whips. Local Kurds traded food for our last coins and my mother's earrings. They were gold earrings with rubies at the center.

The sun rose and fell like a gold coin. Light and shadow leaped from fires at night. Grown-ups talked in a language that I knew but said things I couldn't understand. My grandmother whispered to me, "Hush, hush now. Go to sleep." Sleeping under God's own stars, but God's eyes were elsewhere. Who was watching over us? Who knew where we were going? Who knew where my father was and why a man fell down with blood pouring from his side?

My grandfather trailed behind us, hobbling along with a cane. My mother called back to him, "We'll see you at the resting place." He would arrive after dark and fall down to sleep without even eating. One morning he didn't wake up. My grandmother slapped her face and called out to God in a loud voice. She sat in the dust and wouldn't get up until my mother pulled her to her feet. The next day Grandmother sat down in the dirt by the side of the road and begged us to leave her. She said she couldn't take another step. My mother kissed my grandmother's hands and said a prayer. Then she wrapped a scarf over my head so I couldn't look back.

One morning as we were walking, a rumor passed down the line that the men of Hadjin had been shot on the outskirts of town and buried in a big pit. The women screamed like a flock of starved birds. I put my hands over my ears and hid my face in my mother's shoulder. She didn't make a sound. After that, my mother walked like someone asleep, holding the baby tightly and pushing me ahead of her.

There were bodies everywhere I looked. Some were old, some were babies, some were bleeding from the mouth, some were half-alive. The smell was terrible, the flies, the maggots, the animals chewing on an arm or a leg while the eyes rolled up, staring at the sky. But we kept walking. Where are we going? I asked my mother. She didn't know. But we kept walking.

I saw a mother throw her baby into the river. A Kurdish woman who was washing clothes downstream grabbed the baby from the water. The Kurdish woman took that baby with her— it was almost like the story of Moses in the bulrushes.

My mother sold the pots, the bowls, the spoons, the knife, even her head scarf, for food. All we had left was a tin cup on a frayed string around my neck. A Kurd offered to buy the baby, but my mother wouldn't sell him. I wanted her to sell Krikor so we could get some food, but I felt terrible for thinking this. I thought she should sell me because the Kurd looked like he had a lot of food where he lived. Then I felt worse, because I loved my mother.

We came to a place in the desert where we were told to stay. Krikor died there. At night, under the light of the moon, my mother dug a pit using my cup. She couldn't dig very deep, but she wanted to hide his body from the birds that followed us. She wrapped him in her shawl and put the bundle in the hole. We closed up the place with sand, and then we said a prayer for his soul. The soul of our baby was as small as a breath. It joined the other dead souls in the night wind and blew across the desert sands.

This was to be our home—a stretch of desert. With a large cloth she had taken from a dead woman by the road and some sticks she found, my mother made us a tent. There was just enough room for us to sit up or to lie down side by side on a piece of blanket, with our feet sticking out. I heard someone say, "The name of this place is Ras Al-Ain." We lived there for a while, with barely anything to eat and water I brought in my tin cup, while my mother's eyes grew bigger in her head. She began to look like someone I didn't know.

The day after my mother died, I sat watching the children around me, who were getting ready to go down to the river.

They dug for cool sand, which they put in rags and tied around their feet so the sand wouldn't burn their soles. I had done this every day myself, but I was too tired to do it again. Just then someone shook my shoulder.

"Put these on your feet."

I looked up at a narrow-faced girl who was holding out a pair of rags to me. When I didn't respond, she kneeled down in front of me and began to knot them over my ankles.

"Don't tell me you don't remember me," she said.

It was Arsinee, a girl I knew from our town. Arsinee's father had run a café in Hadjin and one in Mersin, where we went in the summer. She was a little older than me, and a little taller. A few times we had played marbles under a table in the Mersin café while my father and grandfather talked with hers.

"How could I recognize anyone?" I asked. "We all look like dogs."

"My fleas would recognize me anyplace."

I hadn't laughed in so long that it came out like a bark.

"My brother here," said Arsinee, patting a little boy on the head, "has made pets out of his lice."

The boy's belly was sticking out of his tattered shirt like a shelf, but he was smiling. He scratched behind his ear. Suddenly I wanted to run to the river, where I could douse my filthy, tangled hair in the water.

Arsinee continued, "Their names are Bedros, Boghos, and Nubar. There's also a little one called Jesus."

"What if God hears you talking like that?" I asked her.

"God hasn't paid any attention to us in a long time," she said, pulling me to my feet.

Later in the day we walked to the market in town to find something to eat. Arsinee said we had to beg for food.

"My mother would be ashamed if she knew I was begging," I said.

Arsinee said, "In the first place, your mother is dead. In the second place, don't you think she'd be more ashamed if you were dead?"

This made some sense.

"You come begging with us, or lie down and die right here," she said.

So we got a fig, a handful of roasted chickpeas, and a roll. That day we divided the food three ways, and we were always together after that. Arsinee, Sarkis, and I watched out for each other while we were at Ras Al-Ain.

Most days we went into town, to beg in the market or to search the rubbish behind people's houses. Arsinee figured out how to get food for us and made us eat whatever it was. I didn't want to pick the barley kernels out of horse droppings, but Arsinee insisted. I didn't want to eat the lard a woman threw out in the alley, but Arsinee told me if I didn't, she wouldn't let me sleep with her and Sarkis that night. Unfortunately, all three of us were sick after that. The next day we had better luck—a Kurdish woman gave us a half loaf of bread. Someone gave us a handful of bulgur, which we soaked in my cup overnight.

We lived like that for a long time. There weren't any grown-ups left—only children, some of them so small that they didn't know their names. I started to forget what life had been like before, when I had a house and a garden and as much food as I wanted. Sometimes at night I would sing for Arsinee and Sarkis a song my mother taught me, so I could remember her voice. *"Eh leh lepeleh, guz, guz topeleh . . ."* Some nights Arsinee would have bad dreams and wake up shouting. I patted her back until she fell asleep again.

One day on our way to the market, we found a dead and rotting camel by the side of the road. It was filled with squirming maggots and covered with fat black flies. Arsinee used a ragged edge of tin to rip pieces of flesh off the dead thing. She made a little fire and used sticks to roast it, like shish kebab. None of her bullying could get me to eat it, and in the end she didn't have the stomach for it herself.

So we went to the market, where we sat down and sold the meat. We got six pennies, which was a small fortune. With two pennies we bought bread, with two we bought cheese, and we saved the last coins for another day. The food tasted so good, and my belly was full for the first time I could remember since leaving Hadjin.

There were too many children to count at Ras Al-Ain. While we were there, soldiers came and went. English troops were nearby for a while, and some of them were kind. Then they left, and we came under the Turkish government. They put up big tents, and we were divided into boys and girls. Sarkis was small enough that he was allowed to stay with us in a girls' tent. They fed us, except for when the Turkish troops passed through. Then the soldiers were fed first, and we got what was left over, which was usually nothing.

One day we saw an Armenian woman sitting in the market, using a *saj*—a kind of griddle—to cook bread and other things for people. A Turkish boy with a gun and belts of bullets crossed over his chest, like a soldier, told her to hand over the griddle. She needed that *saj*—it was the only way she had of taking care of herself and her family—but she had to give it to him.

Arsinee was ready to jump on the Turk and beat him with all her force, but Sarkis and I grabbed her.

"Let go of me!" she screamed. "I'm going to kill him. I'm going to kill him."

I pulled her arms behind her back, while she tried to kick me and twist free. It was like holding Moug when she wanted to chase down a rat twice her size, straining for a fight she couldn't win. The boy took the *saj* and disappeared into the crowd. Arsinee was so mad, she didn't talk to me, wouldn't look me in the eye even, until the next day.

A week or so later, Arsinee, Sarkis, and I saw that Turk again. He was in our camp, hanging around with some soldiers, and he wasn't wearing a gun, so he looked like any boy.

Arsinee said, "Now's our chance to get him."

"Are you crazy?" I said to her. "There are soldiers everyplace here."

She laughed. "That's why we can do it. I'll trip him when he walks by, you and Sarkis hold him down, and I'm going to beat him. Then we run away, hide behind the soldiers' tent. He's a coward, and he'll be too ashamed to do anything. What kind of a Turk lets little kids beat him up?"

"I won't do it," I said. But in my mind's eye, I could see myself pressing his arms to the ground.

It happened exactly the way she said. Sarkis and I pinned his arms down, while Arsinee sat on his stomach and hit his head. Then we ran like sand beetles and got away. That night, when we were settling down in a corner of the tent, Arsinee asked, "Now don't you feel good?" I did feel good. I felt even better the next day when I saw his black eye.

Weeks followed weeks, the sun and the moon circling in their familiar patterns. Then one day the soldiers divided us into groups and took bunches of children off in caravans. Each day three or four tents would be gone. We heard they were taking the orphans to Stamboul, and Arsinee and I decided to go, as if we had any choice. Finally they took down our tent and loaded us into a wagon for the journey.

The last part of the trip was over the cobbled streets of the city. We pressed against the slats of the wagon to see the minarets and domes of the mosques. Arsinee and I ended up in a Turkish orphanage for girls, and Sarkis was in the boys' section on the other side of the wall. When we arrived, they shaved our hair for lice, washed us with stinging soap, and gave us cotton dresses. We lined up in the courtyard and were given

Turkish names. Mine was Neriman. And Arsinee was Elif. We weren't supposed to speak Armenian anymore.

The directress was strict, but if you followed the rules, you were okay. We learned how to read, write, and sing songs in Turkish and to add and subtract. We worked part of the day knitting slippers, which were sold in the market. We also helped in the kitchen and cleaned the orphanage. The worst job was scrubbing the floors with brushes on hands and knees.

We had food, a place to lay our heads each night, and a roof to keep off the rain. But Arsinee was unhappy. She didn't want to be called Elif. She wanted to go to Mersin, a seaside town where she thought her uncle's family was still living. Nobody cared if we left or stayed, so she waited until she had saved up enough food for her and Sarkis, a little bit each day, to make the trip. I thought she was crazy to give up bread and shelter, without knowing if her family was still there, but Arsinee was stubborn.

The evening before she left, we were sitting in the court-yard by the well. She took the tin cup from my pocket and dipped it in the water.

"Come over here," she ordered.

When I went to her, she grabbed my head and poured the water over it. "Now you're baptized into our family. We'll send for you if we can."

There was water dripping down my face, and I saw she was crying. I filled the cup again and poured it over her hair.

The water mixed with her tears. We put our two foreheads together. We sang, *"Eh leh, lepeleh, guz, guz, topeleh . . ."*

When they left the next morning, Sarkis clung to my dress, and we had to unpeel his fingers from my hem. But Arsinee and I, our hearts were as hard as month-old bread. Her eyes were on the road to Mersin. And I knew I'd have to be tough like Arsinee to get along without her.

After they disappeared around the corner, I turned back from the gate. Then I drank water from my cup until I was full.

CHAPTER TWO

Armenian Eyes

(ISTANBUL, 1924)

One night soon after Arsinee left, I was lying on my sleeping mat, listening to the sounds of the dark room. The girl next to me whispered in Armenian, "Are you awake?" Though it was forbidden, Arsinee and I had sometimes spoken in Armenian to each other when no one else was near. There were other Armenian girls at the orphanage, but Arsinee and I stayed to ourselves. Now I was alone. The girl asked again, "Are you awake?" I didn't want any trouble, so I answered in Turkish, "I'm sleeping."

I felt like a branch torn from a tree. The river swept me along, and I kept afloat as best I could. There was food every day. My hands were busy knitting, scouring pots, sweeping floors. I knew the names of the other girls but wasn't a particular friend to any of them. I also made no enemies. The teacher liked me because my handwriting was neat and I didn't raise my voice, except to sing patriotic Turkish songs when it was required.

In the orphanage, as a girl's body changed and she wasn't a child anymore, she moved from the middle room to the upper room. We watched each other carefully for telltale signs and tried to guess who would be the next among us to make the move. Finally the day came that I carried my bedding up the stairs. I was proud that I was no longer a child but frightened about what would happen.

The only place to go from the upper room was out into the world—as a servant, an apprentice, or a wife to a poor man, because no one else would marry a penniless orphan. A couple of times a week, someone came to the place looking for a worker or a wife. I would take one look at the man, curl myself into an awkward shape, and edge to the back of the line. Some other girl would be chosen and march off with a tailor or baker, never to be seen again. Then there would be discussion among the older girls about whether the life a girl had gone to was likely to be terrible or not.

One day a man came looking for a household servant. His clothes were fine, and he carried a walking stick with a gold handle. He seemed like a nice man, so I jostled my way to the front. I stood straight and held my face like a flower turned to the sun. He walked down the line, speaking with each girl in turn.

"What's your name?" he asked me.

"Neriman," I answered. I had nothing clever to say, so I looked directly at him before lowering my eyes.

"Neriman," he repeated.

By then years had gone by since Arsinee left, and no word from her had come. I didn't know if she and Sarkis had made it to Mersin. I never really believed Arsinee would be able to send for me. Who would want another orphan, and one that wasn't a blood relation? I went with no regrets with Aziz *Effendi* to be a kitchen maid in his house.

Luck was with me again, because the Aziz were kind people. They had two other girls working in the house. Emine, the girl who looked after the children, had a wonderful voice for singing, and the children loved her. She and I got along well. Sarmin, the girl who cleaned the house, was dull witted and jealous. Sometimes she snuck into the kitchen and added wood to the flames so the pots boiled over. I had to watch her from the corners of my eyes.

Ummahan, the old cook, was half-blind and toothless. She rattled the copper pots, banged the bowls, and grumbled as she cooked, but she was kind to me. The first time I was alone in the pantry at the Aziz house, I stuffed myself with plump golden figs. My stomach gurgled and swelled like a drum. I was sick the next day, but no one said anything.

By the end of four weeks in that household, I was no longer a scrawny chicken. During the next months Ummahan taught me enough that I was able to take over the preparation of meals. She sat in the back courtyard, snoozing in the sun, and the kitchen was mine.

It was the custom for the women of the household to go together to the baths for the entire day. Emine, Sarmin, and I accompanied our mistress, while the children stayed at home with Ummahan. Washing was only a small part of what went on at the baths—we also brought sewing and embroidery. I packed a lunch basket for our midday meal. The mistress would gossip with her cousins and friends.

One particular bath day, after I had been with the Aziz for most of a year, I met someone who would alter my life once again. When we reached the *hammam*, we exchanged our clothes for big white linen wrappers, resting our belongings on low-lying benches along one corner of the bathing hall. I dipped my feet in a channel of warm water that passed through the tiled floor and sat on a stool near one of the fountains in the middle of the room. We scrubbed and wrung out our washcloths in water basins. The room filled with steam, and voices echoed off the tiled walls.

Soon it was so hot, sweat ran down my forehead in little rivers, stinging my eyes with salt. The damp air burned my nostrils. When I asked the mistress for permission to move to the anteroom, she agreed. In the cooling room, I sat on a cushioned bench with my eyes closed and my head resting on the tiled wall. Behind my eyelids, I saw my mother pouring a basin of water over my head at the baths in Hadjin. I was a small child with long hair down my back. There was laughter; someone was singing. I heard a woman's voice speaking in Armenian and felt pressure on my arm.

When I opened my eyes, a strange woman with gold bracelets ringing her bare arms asked me something in Armenian. I stared at her in silence. Her dark eyes were fringed with long lashes. She had a prominent nose, a well-cut mouth, and a thick braid over her shoulder, with short tendrils of hair curling at her temples. I saw my face reflected in the woman's eyes: an oval framed by dark hair, my eyes shining black.

The woman asked in Turkish, "My dear, are you Armenian?"

I said, "No. I'm Turkish."

The woman took hold of my right forearm and turned it up. A blue cross, with the date 1914 at one end, proved that I had lied. I was very young when my parents had taken me to Jerusalem on a pilgrimage. A man just outside the walls of the Armenian monastery had given me and my mother the same tattoos. There was another tattoo—the head of John the Baptist surrounded by a garden fence—on my other arm.

"Dear," the woman whispered, "I am Armenian. *Yes hay em.* And I want to help you."

"*Hanum,* the people I serve treat me well." My heart was like a rabbit caught in human hands. I saw Sarmin in the doorway, staring at us. I raised my eyebrows at her, and she scurried out. I was sure she was running to tattle.

The Armenian woman said quietly, "There are many children like you who have been taken into Turkish homes. What is your name?"

"My Turkish name is Neriman, but my parents called me Zabelle." *Yes hay em,* I thought. The words echoed up through a deep well.

"Zabelle, I know of several Armenian families who are taking in orphans like you. Tell me the name of your master and the street on which you live, and we will save you."

For a minute I thought about lying. If I told her the truth, I might fall into worse circumstances. I looked at the tattoos on my arms again. I whispered the address to the woman and ran back to the other room.

I joined Emine, and after taking the comb from her, I began untangling her wet hair. I saw Sarmin whispering to Hava *Hanum.* Their heads were so close, they almost touched.

"Neriman," called Hava *Hanum.* "Come here."

I went to my mistress. Sarmin smirked at me. I would have pinched her if she had been within reach.

"Neriman, were you speaking to a strange woman in the cooling room?"

"No, *Hanum.*"

"Are you sure, dear? Sarmin said she saw you."

"No, *Hanum*. I spoke with no one."

I don't think the mistress believed me, because she insisted we pack up without taking lunch. We hurried to the changing rooms and swept out of the bath.

When I prepared the evening meal, I was so nervous that I had to remind myself what I was cooking. Would the woman from the bath send people to save me? Where would they take me?

When Sarmin came into the room to fetch a broom, she said, "Neriman, the sweat on your lip is about to drop into the food."

"If you're not careful, traitor," I said, the knife heavy in my hand, "your nose might fall in." I leaned toward Sarmin, grasping her sleeve, but she wrested her arm away and ran out of the kitchen.

I carved the innards out of eggplants, tomatoes, and green peppers for *dolma*. The blade slipped close to my fingers several times. Soon the kitchen filled with the smells of simmering vegetables, onions, lamb, and cracked wheat. I made *ghadayif* for dessert, because it was the *Effendi*'s favorite.

When the mistress peered into the kitchen, I pretended not to see her. I chopped walnuts, the knife giving a satisfying whack as it bit into the board. I wondered how long it would take the Armenian woman to send someone for me.

* * *

"Yes, my girl, you have learned well. This food will give us all long life and good health." Aziz *Effendi* was full of praise for my cooking.

I went back to the kitchen to eat with Emine and Sarmin. I did a good imitation of the master, rubbing my belly and burping while I talked, until all three of us were laughing so hard, we could barely breathe. I decided to forgive Sarmin, because I'd never have to see her again.

When we went to bed that night, Sarmin fell asleep immediately. Emine and I stayed awake whispering for a while.

"What happened at the bath?" Emine asked.

"Sarmin made up some story that upset the mistress," I said.

It was too bad I couldn't tell her the truth. I liked Emine. I closed my eyes and saw the letters of my real name.

"Neriman, are you asleep?" she asked.

I didn't answer.

Under the bright sun, I walked in the desert, my feet wrapped in sand-filled rags. In my tin cup I carried water for my mother, who lay sick in the tent. I marched and marched, but the sand seemed to stretch and grow under my feet, until the tent was a small black dot on the horizon.

"Neriman! Wake up." Emine jostled me out of sleep. "It's time to get up. Go make breakfast." She ran out, heading for the children's rooms upstairs.

Sunlight streamed in the high window, making a patch on the end of my pallet on the floor. I flung off the blanket and lay staring at the ceiling. For the midday meal we needed tomatoes and olives from the market. And I should remind *Hanum* about coal for the stove. Maybe the Armenians weren't coming after all.

Later in the day I was in the upstairs hall, putting away the clean kitchen linens. I heard a loud knock at the front door. I felt as though I had been caught stealing the master's coins, and I wanted to climb into the cupboard and hide. Aziz *Effendi* opened the door, but from the top of the stairs I couldn't see who had knocked or hear what was being said.

"Neriman! Neriman, come here," my master called.

I went slowly down the stairs. In the entrance hall there was a bearded priest dressed in black robes and a black peaked hood, standing before the master. The priest was old, but just behind him were three tall young priests.

"Girl," Aziz *Effendi* said kindly, "these men say you are Armenian. If you are, they are here to bring you back to your people."

The old man came toward me and put his hand on my shoulder. He asked me in Armenian, *"Aghchig, mayr, hayr unis?"*

This is my language, I thought, and these are my people. He was asking if I had a mother and a father, and I answered truthfully in Armenian, *"Voch."* I stared at my slippers, unable to look at either Aziz *Effendi* or the old man.

"What is your name, child?" he asked.

In Armenian I answered, "My name is Zabelle."

The priest smiled and nodded to his companions. He said to the master in Turkish, "So, this lamb is one of ours, and with your permission, *Effendi,* we will take her with us now."

"Go to your room and pack your things, Neriman. Say good-bye to *Hanum* and the children," Aziz *Effendi* said. "We will miss this girl," he told the Armenians. "She is a fine cook."

I tied up my few clothes in a shawl. In a cloth bag I put my hairpins, comb, and the tin cup, which had come with me from Hadjin. I looked at my pale face in a small hand mirror the mistress had given me, then slid the mirror into the bag. Like a cat, I was about to leap from one life to another, trusting only my instincts, with very little idea of where I would land.

As I stepped out into the street, the old priest took my hand.

"Zabelle, my child, we'll go back to the church for tonight. *Digin* Der Stepanian, the woman you met at the bath yesterday, may take you in. First thing tomorrow, we will see the magistrate, who decides if we were right to take you as one of our flock." He spoke to me in Turkish, for he understood without asking that I remembered very little Armenian.

We walked down the dark cobbled street, with the priest's men on either side. I had to trot to keep up with them. When I turned back to look at the Aziz house, I saw a group of men following closely behind. I glanced over my shoulder again, and now there were even more men at our heels. Night had fallen, and I couldn't make out the faces. A few lanterns cast long dark shadows on the buildings we passed. I bowed my head, and tears started running down my face as I hurried along next to the priest.

He stopped and looked into my face. "My dear girl, there's no need to be afraid. Those are Armenian men who joined us on our way when they found out we were going to save an Armenian girl. You are safe now with your people."

When we arrived, the priest gestured that I should enter through a wooden gate into the courtyard. We went into the priests' quarters, where an old serving woman dressed in black named *Digin* Takouhi took charge of me. The priest told her to speak to me in Turkish. She showed me to a small room near the kitchen.

The priest was the Patriarch of Constantinople, she told me. It was because he was the leader of all Armenians in the region that the Aziz had let me go.

"You are lucky, *aghchigs,* because there are many Armenian girls who were stolen away—some of them were made wives to Kurds, some of them worse, and I can't use the words for what happened to our virgins during the deportations. Not to mention the thousands of martyrs lost in the desert, your own parents among them. The Turks massacred our people." The old woman shook her head and glanced up at the ceiling.

"Why, O Lord, do you test your people so mightily? For which of our sins is all this pain?"

I was sitting on the mat, unbraiding my hair, while she talked. Her words fell around me like rain on dry, hard ground. It was the first time I had heard anyone describe what had happened to us, and I didn't know how to think about it.

"We lost too many to count, but tonight we took back one of our lambs, and we thank God for each one returned to the fold. Good night, dear. May the Lord watch over your sleep."

After *Digin* Takouhi had shuffled down the hall, I put out the light and dropped immediately to sleep.

I walked across the desert toward the tent, carrying the tin cup filled with water for my sick mother. The sun was hot and bright. The sand shifted under my feet, but I struggled on. As I neared the tent, I called, "Mayrig!" There was no response. When I tried to run, my feet sank even deeper into the sand, but finally I reached the tent and flung open its flap. My mother was gone. I fell to my knees, tore back the blanket, and plunged my hands into the sand. I pulled up bone after bone: leg bones, arm bones, ribs, and finally a skull with rubies for eyes.

I sat up in bed. My hands trembled as I tied back my damp hair with a rag. I lay down and shut my eyes against the dark. Softly in Armenian, I began to recite begats from Genesis. The verses came back to me, rising from somewhere inside my body. *Now these are the generations of the sons of Noah, Shem, Ham,* and *Japheth: and unto them were sons born after the flood. . . .*

When I couldn't remember any more names from the Bible, I said the other names I remembered, the names of the lost.

In the morning I helped *Digin* Takouhi prepare breakfast for the Patriarch and the other priests. When *Digin* went to serve them, I swept the kitchen floor. The old woman shuffled into the room, carrying an empty tray.

"Well, dear," she said, "it seems you are going to see the judge this afternoon, and tomorrow morning the Der Stepanians are coming to take you home. *Baron* Der Stepanian was here already this morning, speaking with His Holiness. You are fortunate to be going to that house; they are good people."

Again I had jumped and managed to land on my feet.

"Do they have children?" I asked.

"Three children—two boys and a girl. The girl is about your age.

"And servants?" I wondered what my position would be.

"Yes. But you'll be like one of the family until you've grown a bit and they find you a husband. If they can't find you one, you may go back to being a cook, but not, praise God, for the Turks."

"A kitchen is a kitchen." I smiled, and at that *Digin* Takouhi laughed.

"Well, dear, some kitchens are *Christian*," she said.

* * *

When I left with the Patriarch and his men to go see the judge, I wore a new dress, new stockings, and beautiful leather shoes that had been sent by the Der Stepanians. The dress was blue cotton with a black stripe, and the lace-up shoes were black. It was a sunny day, but not too hot, and as we walked through the open markets, I was happy. In my pocket were three coins that the Patriarch had given me.

As we entered the building that led to the judge's chamber, the Patriarch said to me, "Listen, my child, the judge is going to determine if you are Armenian or not. Since you don't speak much Armenian—which would be proof enough—he's going to ask you some questions, but it shouldn't take more than a few minutes."

The judge told me to come up to the desk behind which he was sitting. "So, what is your name, child?"

"Do you want to know my Armenian name or my Turkish name?" I asked in Turkish. It occurred to me that I could offer to write Zabelle in Armenian. Or I could roll up my sleeves and show him the tattoos.

He laughed. "Never mind, my dear, neither. I can tell by your eyes that you are Armenian." After a few respectful words to the Patriarch, he sent us out.

When we were in the street again, the Patriarch put his hand on my shoulder and said, "Now, my dear, you must relearn your language." Out of his pocket he pulled an Armenian Bible, which he handed to me. "Start with the beginning," he said.

* * *

I dreamed of the desert that night. Dusk had fallen, and I carried my tin cup filled with water across the sand. When I reached the black tent, my mother was gone, but there was a baby asleep on a carpet. I picked up the baby and offered it some water. The baby's eyes were large and dark and filled with sadness. When the infant began to cry, I carried it out of the tent. In the night sky, a chipped moon appeared through passing clouds. With the baby on my hip, I began the long walk toward the lights of a distant town.

CHAPTER THREE

The Balcony

(CONSTANTINOPLE, 1924–1926)

When I arrived at the Der Stepanians' home, I thought I had walked into the sultan's palace or the castle of the king of France. A crystal chandelier lit up the entrance hall, where an enormous tapestry of animals in a forest hung along the wall. There were deep red-and-burgundy Persian carpets over every inch of the floor. A servant gave me a pair of embroidered velvet slippers, and my shoes were whisked away to be cleaned.

I found out later that *Baron* Der Stepanian owned a business that exported carpets to France. The family had lived in Paris during the war, and when they came back, they brought French furniture and a phonograph with them. In their house I learned Armenian again and picked up a little French as well. *Je m'appelle Zabelle.*

That first afternoon *Digin* Der Stepanian led me by the hand up the stairs and showed me to my room, which had a tall bed and a balcony overlooking the street. She asked me to call her *Mayrig*. The word wouldn't come out of my mouth, so I called her Auntie instead. She studied me with big, pity-filled eyes, as though I were the last orphan dragged half-dead from the desert.

After she left I sat in the middle of the bed, which felt like a cushioned board on stilts. Then I opened the wardrobe, where I found seven dresses in my size, cotton stockings that matched the dresses, and neatly folded sets of underclothes edged with lace. The clothes were beautiful, but they worried me.

I wasn't a servant, and I wasn't a Der Stepanian. Like a distant cousin from the countryside, I had to be dressed properly and taught manners, except that we shared no blood. I was an honored houseguest, who had done nothing to deserve the honor. Where else was there for me to go? I would have to be careful. That first night when I lay down in the French bed, I was afraid I would roll off in my sleep, waking everyone with a loud thud. So I pulled off the blankets and slept on the rug.

Dalita Der Stepanian was about my age. Stepan and Barkev were younger and spent most of their days at school, but Dalita and I didn't go out much. We went to church on Sundays and to the baths with Auntie. Three mornings a week

I had Armenian lessons with a white-bearded priest. A woman from the church came twice a week to teach me and Dalita to work lace and to embroider. Dalita's lace was such a mess of different-sized knots and loops that the woman gave up and we concentrated on embroidery. Even this was taxing for Dalita, though, so I finished off most of the pieces she started.

Sometimes Auntie's sisters and cousins would stop by for tea, or we would go to their houses. But most afternoons Dalita and I brushed and braided each other's hair. She gave me a pair of tortoiseshell combs, and we borrowed necklaces and bracelets from her mother. We played the phonograph—only the saddest music, about people suffering from love. We wore scarves at our waists and danced across the carpet in our velvet slippers. Dalita adored the French singers because she had fallen in love with a boy in France and claimed her heart would never mend. I liked the Turkish songs, which were filled with melancholy and passion.

I spent a lot of time in my bedroom, staring out the balcony window down onto the street. One beautiful spring day I opened the glass door and the wooden shutter and moved a stool out onto the balcony. The sun was hot on my face, and the air was breezy and fresh. Before long the facing neighbor sent a servant to report to Auntie that I was displaying myself like a harlot. Of course, Auntie didn't use these words when she asked me not to sit on the balcony, but one of the maids told me later.

Time went by. Although it was never discussed, I knew I was not meant to live with the Der Stepanians forever. They figured that I was around sixteen years old, which seemed to me like the time to get married. But I was without dowry, without family, and would have to depend on the Der Stepanians to find me a husband. It wasn't for me to say anything, so I waited for them to bring it up.

I didn't know any men, except for the *Baron* and the gardener. So when I daydreamed about a husband, it was in the vaguest terms. Would he be rich? Would he be poor? Young or old? Would he have a mustache and a pocket watch? Would he smell like tobacco or peppermint oil?

One afternoon I was standing inside the balcony window, holding the curtain to one side, staring down at the street. Each man who passed in the street I considered as a possible husband. This one was too fat, that one too old. A group of students went by, carrying their satchels filled with papers and books. They looked too young. Then the peanut seller, who peddled his wares on our street at the end of the day, came along. He was thin as a reed, browned by the sun, and very handsome. Suddenly he was looking straight up at me. I jumped back from the window.

The next day I waited for him to pass, and sure enough, he waved up at me, although he couldn't possibly have seen me through the lace curtains. Every day I watched for him. He gazed up at my window as he went by, and before he rounded the bend of our street, he'd cast back a glance. Soon I began to pull back the curtain slightly, so he could see me. I checked all the neighbors' facing windows before I did this.

My whole being leaned toward the moment in the late afternoon when he would be beneath my window. When I closed my eyes while the phonograph played, I imagined I was Leyla, and it was his voice singing, *"Desires with longing are sacrificed, Leyla. If I die before my love fills your heart, This is the bitterness of separation my soul, Leyla. . . ."*

"Greetings, my beautiful one!" he shouted up at me one day.

I grabbed the wooden shutters and pulled them closed. Even though my heart was thumping like a rabbit in a box, the sound of his laughter made me smile.

There was a knock on my door. Could the neighbor have gotten news across the street that fast? I didn't think so. It was Auntie.

"Zabelle, sweetheart," she said, "I've been wanting to talk with you. Come into my room."

I followed her across the hall to her chamber, where we sat on a long sofa. She was so lovely, with her blue black hair and long curling eyelashes. There were lines at the corners of her mouth, and a few around her eyes, but she would be beautiful even as an old woman.

"It seems that you are now of an age to consider marriage, dear," she said.

I nodded in agreement.

"Well, someone has approached my husband to ask for your hand."

I immediately thought of the peanut boy. But he was too poor. He would never dare talk to *Baron* Der Stepanian.

Auntie continued. "It was *Baron* Seferian."

I wanted to faint. I knew who he was. He had stopped to talk with the Der Stepanians as we were leaving church several weeks in a row. The bony, long-toothed spice merchant who had hair sprouting from his nose and was almost bald. I was sure he would smell as musty as ground turmeric.

"He is a childless widower, dear, and could take good care of you."

I tried to be calm. A childless widower, a spice merchant with a big house and many servants, a man who would take care of me. Old enough to be my grandfather, with big yellow teeth and hair on the knuckles of his hands. Auntie couldn't really mean for me to marry him.

"Auntie," I asked, "Isn't he old enough to be your father?"

"Sweetheart, you're so pretty, and bright, that it's a shame for you to be married to someone so old. But without family, without dowry, or prospects . . . I don't know what we'll be able to find."

I stared at the toes of my slippers.

She sighed. "We'll tell him no."

I prayed, and prayed, and prayed that the next offer would be a better one, because it was one I couldn't refuse. In the meantime I kept up my afternoon meetings with the boy from the street. I got bolder because I knew time was short. He offered me a bag of nuts, and I leaned over the railing as he tossed them up to me. He begged me to tell him my name. I just laughed.

One afternoon Auntie asked me to pour tea for a guest I hadn't met before. Vartanoush Chahasbanian was, Auntie explained, a distant relative of hers from Adana. I didn't pay much attention to the woman. There were all sorts of people in and out of the house in the afternoons, and she must have been a very distant relation, because I'd never heard mention of her before. That evening Auntie raised one of her crescent-shaped eyebrows at me and told me that *Digin* Chahasbanian was looking for a wife for her son. The son lived in America, and *Digin* and the lucky girl would be leaving in a matter of weeks to join him.

So this was it. *Digin* Chahasbanian would stop by again later in the week, as I had passed the initial inspection. It went without saying that if she wanted me for her son, I was theirs.

When she returned, I studied Vartanoush Chahasbanian from under my lashes and out the sides of my eyes as she and Auntie talked. Dalita, who knew the story, stared at the woman and kept checking for my reaction. My future mother-in-law, I said to myself. Her white hair was pulled into a bun at the top of her head, her mouth was drawn up like a string purse, and she dressed in widow's black with a simple gold chain around her neck. When she talked about her son, Toros, it was clear that she was proud.

She handed a photograph to Auntie, who passed it to me. I looked at it for a moment. His hair was parted on the side, with gray at the temples. The ears stuck out a little, but it was a handsome face. He wore a suit, with a vest and a tie, and the shoes were gleaming. Definitely a better match than old Seferian. I thought *Digin* Chahasbanian might find me rude if I studied the picture too long, so I passed it to Dalita.

When Auntie showed her cousin to the door, Dalita turned on the phonograph. French love songs. She said, "He doesn't look bad, but I don't want you to go to America."

That was the part I liked best about the prospect, but I didn't tell Dalita. That night I lay in my bed, thinking, This is my husband, Toros Chahasbanian. My name is Zabelle Chahasbanian. And America! A new country, an ocean away from what had been lost.

All the arrangements were made. My papers, the marriage by proxy—so when I left Constantinople I would already be a married woman—and the trunk I would need for the clothes and things the Der Stepanians had given me. *Digin* Chahasbanian wanted a picture of me to send to her son. It wasn't sure that the photograph would get there before we did, but still I went to the studio to sit on a big chair in front of a dark screen.

For the picture, I wore an ivory silk dress with a beaded flower on one shoulder, a dropped waist, and lace all around the hem. That was Auntie's going-away gift to me. My satin shoes matched the dress. I had on a double strand of pearls that Auntie loaned to me and the combs from Dalita. The exploding flash scared me, but I kept a smile on my face.

Every afternoon I waited for the peanut seller. The summer was almost over, and the days were getting shorter. We never talked much—how could you talk from the balcony without shouting into the street? We just waved to each other, smiled, said a few words. I knew he was called Berj, but I still hadn't told him my name. He was the kind of handsome that seemed dangerous, with a crooked smile and black eyes.

It was a pity he was poor. He had a very hard life, carrying his wares up and down the streets. Who knew where he lived. I must have looked like a princess to him, in that elegant house, wearing fancy dresses, with no work required of me. He couldn't have known that I was an impostor, not rich at all, but an orphan living on someone's goodwill.

The final day before my departure, I finished packing the trunk. On the very top was my tin cup from Hadjin, the only thing that remained from my family's home. After the clasps on the lid had been snapped shut, I tied a red velvet ribbon to a lock of hair in the back of my head, close to my neck, and clipped it off with the scissors. I wrote on one of Auntie's scented notes, "Tomorrow I go to America. May the light be with you." In a small scarf I knotted the hair, the note, and three gold coins. Maybe he couldn't read, but someone could read it for him.

It was nearing dusk when he came by, and I was waiting on the balcony, looking at this street in Constantinople for the last time. I saw the mistress of the neighboring house peer out at me from her window, but I didn't care.

"Berj," I called, "this is for you." I tossed the small bundle down to him.

He caught it and brought it to his lips, then thrust it inside his shirt. "Thank you, O nameless beauty!" He dropped to his knees in the middle of the street, almost upsetting his tray.

"Get up, you crazy fool." I laughed. "My name is Zabelle."

"Zabelle!" he shouted. "Zabelle, the lovely, the queen of sunset and summer and angels. O merciful God, thank you for blessing this day with Zabelle!"

Just then the neighbor flung open her window and screeched at me, "Get back in the house, you shameless hussy! And you," she shouted down at Berj, "I'm going to get the police after you!"

He flashed his crooked smile at me, then sped down the street and out of sight. I shut the balcony door behind me, and went to find Auntie in case the neighbor's maid was already on her way across the street.

The next morning breakfast was a somber affair. Red-eyed Dalita sat next to me and rested her head on my shoulder. I put my arm around her waist but felt as though I had already departed.

The Der Stepanians accompanied me and *Digin* Chahasbanian to the pier. Dalita gave me a handkerchief she had embroidered herself. Auntie was crying and promised that she would write to me. *Digin* Chahasbanian and I climbed the ship's ramp. As the ship headed out to sea, I stood at the rail with my new mother-in-law, watching the city of Constantinople grow smaller and more distant. Across the ocean, my new husband and my American life were waiting.

CHAPTER FOUR

Holy War

(WATERTOWN, 1927)

I stood on the ship's deck, watching the lace-topped waves roll by. The salt wind blew strands of loose hair in my face and pulled on the edges of the thick shawl I wore over my coat. The ocean spread so far and wide in all directions that I felt like a grain of sand in God's shoe. Below deck, the old woman was ashen faced and miserable. I brought her water, crackers, and thin soups, which were the only things she could keep down. She asked me to read from Psalms, while she lay on her bed with her eyes closed. When she slept, I finished embroidering red plums on a pair of wedding towels I had begun at the Der Stepanians.

We came into the country through Ellis Island in New York. Bigger and busier than the Istanbul bazaar, the hall was filled with people speaking languages I'd never heard before. On solid ground, my mother-in-law's color improved, and she pushed her way through lines and questions without uttering a word of English or bowing her head.

Soon we were on a train bound for Boston, where Toros Chahasbanian—my husband and her son—was waiting for us. Outside the window, ice-slicked trees and white fields dotted with pastel wooden houses sped by. It was a new world for me, and my eyes were wide. But my mother-in-law sat opposite me, brooding like a disgruntled hen. Every time I glanced away from the window, she was staring at me with suspicion and distaste. I could tell she was having second thoughts about having chosen me for her son, but what could she do now?

As for me, I still thought an unknown husband in America was preferable to the spice merchant that I left behind in Constantinople. Vartanoush Chahasbanian was a lint picker, but I was young and full of hope. I was sure I could win her over.

Once she started talking, my mother-in-law didn't stop. She launched into a series of lessons on household management, towel folding, and the proper way to conduct oneself as a young wife. I was expected to sit and nod my head, taking it all in like a water pitcher. When she started reciting a recipe for *cheoregs,* my pride got the best of me. As a cook for the Aziz, I had learned a few tricks of my own and wanted to impress her.

"If you add a little sugar to the yeast and water, the dough will rise better," I said.

"What?" demanded my mother-in-law. "Is the baby bird now to teach the mother bird to fly? I, who have been making *cheoregs* since before your parents even thought of you, I am being told how to make dough rise?" Her face was as red as a tomato, and it looked like her head was going to pop off from the pressure of her blood.

I lowered my eyes and stared at my innocent, folded hands. Any Armenian will tell you that the Turks have the best curses, and I was running my mind over a string of choice Turkish insults for the likes of Vartanoush Chahasbanian. When I glanced up through my lashes, she was staring at me with smoke pouring out of her ears and nostrils. It was as though she could hear my thoughts or see the phrases passing over my face, and her anger was about to set the train compartment on fire.

Then she reached out and slapped me with all her might. Her palm scorched its print into my cheek. I felt my teeth shift in my head and tears smart into my eyes. I wouldn't give her the satisfaction, though, of seeing me cry. It occurred to me that if Auntie had known what a beast this woman was, she might have let me marry the peanut seller.

When the train pulled into the station, I searched the crowd for my husband. I spotted him at the same moment that his mother began wailing, "My son! My son!" He was clean shaven and modern in a brown suit and an overcoat, with white hairs at his temples, and ears that I recognized from the photo.

"Mayrig!" he called, trying to push his way to the front of the crowd. His breath ballooned on the frozen air.

"My son!" Vartanoush gingerly climbed down the steps and into his arms. I was left to heft our bags to the platform. I waited until they separated from their embrace. Toros looked at me, and I dipped my head in greeting.

His mother flicked the back of her hand at me. "Yes, son, this is the wife I brought you." She sighed. "This is Zabelle."

I looked at him closely. There was no trace of his mother's malice in his eyes. His face was handsome. He was old, but not so old. He was Toros Chahasbanian, American grocer. My husband.

"This," Toros said, turning the knob and pushing open the door, "is the water closet." He pulled a chain on the toilet, and water came churning down a pipe into the bowl.

Vartanoush was impressed by all the conveniences in our new second-floor apartment: the water closet, the icebox, the modern stove. Steam heat clanged from radiators in each room, keeping the whole place summer warm in the dead of winter. Sun streamed in the high windows, and the furniture was spare, making the place feel very large. The apartment

lacked a woman's touch, but Vartanoush took from her bags
lace doilies for the armchairs and a lace runner for the side-
board. Then she started dinner, over Toros's protests that she
should rest.

I went to the bedroom I would share with Toros and
unpacked my bag. His things filled the tallboy by the door, but
he had left the dresser empty. In the top drawer I arranged my
precious things: the tin cup, a small hand mirror, a set of tortoiseshell hair combs, two pair of gloves, a hatpin, and a Bible.
There was space in the closet for my dresses, and he had pushed
his shoes to one side to make room for mine. Out the window,
I could see a neighbor's clothesline, with frozen white shirts
swaying in the wind.

That evening we sat down to the dinner that Vartanoush
had prepared. She was a terrible cook. The pilaf was dry and
tasteless, the lamb and bean stew was oversalted and over-
cooked. Even the coffee she scalded. Toros, who had second
helpings, swallowed it all down without a word. I wondered if
he ate so heartily out of love for his mother or if he had lost his
sense of taste.

Then we sat in the living room. I was silent as a doorknob, while mother and son caught up on six years of news.
They discussed friends and neighbors who had survived the
war, trading names that meant nothing to me. I watched the
hands move round the clock face and started feeling nervous
as it grew later. There was that big bed in our bedroom, and I
knew that something would happen in it.

Now, Armenian women are very modest. And all unmarried Armenian women and girls are virgins, even the ones who are not. And I was. No adult had ever explained to me about how babies are made, but in the orphanage I had heard a few things. Then there had been occasional hints from *Digin* Der Stepanian and jokes from some of the women at the baths. I had a notion of what it was to be husband and wife. I studied Toros's face, wondering how it would feel when he kissed me. I looked over at Vartanoush, who pursed her mouth and raised a skeptical eyebrow. How was it possible that she could read my mind?

Finally Toros checked his pocket watch and announced that it was time. In the hallway we parted ways. Vartanoush marched into her bedroom like a defeated general. Toros went into the bathroom. And I went into our bedroom to wait.

There was a beautiful, white silk nightdress on the bed. Toros had left it there for me. I hung my clothes and underthings over a chair in the corner and slid on the nightgown. It was so long that the fabric pooled at my feet. I undid the pins that held my hair in a coil, lay down in the bed, and spread the hair into a fan across the pillow.

The room was dark, and then the door opened. Toros shut out the wedge of light that fell in behind him. He climbed into his side of the bed. The two of us lay side by side, under the same thick blanket, listening to each other breathe. Then Toros reached out and touched my shoulder.

I remembered Berj, my beautiful street peddler. He called for me to come down from the balcony, and I went.

* * *

The next morning while Toros was still sleeping, I tiptoed out of the room. I washed and dressed in the bathroom and went into the kitchen, where Vartanoush sat at the kitchen table.

She gestured at me to sit down and poured out a cup of tea. "So, now you're a married woman," my mother-in-law said. She stirred her tea, clinking the spoon noisily.

I wished it were my own mother sitting across from me, or Auntie Der Stepanian. I wasn't going to say anything to that nosy woman who didn't wish me well. If she had her way, I'd have been sleeping in the front stairwell. So I kept my mouth shut.

She said, with hatred in her eyes, "You know the old proverb, 'In a house with two mistresses, the floor will never be swept.' This house has one mistress, and you're looking at her."

It was a declaration of war.

Toros came into the kitchen. "Good morning, Mother. Good morning, Zabelle." He paused briefly behind me, his fingertips resting on the back of my chair, then he sat down.

If she wanted war, there would be fighting. And a cat can't catch mice while wearing gloves.

Toros left for the store. Vartanoush covered her hair with an old scarf to start cleaning the house. She handed me a bucket and a scrub brush and told me to wash the kitchen floor. I hadn't so much as lifted a finger in the Der Stepanian house, and now

I was to get down on my hands and knees in dirty water. But I did what was asked.

As I dragged the brush over the linoleum, I thought about my new life. If only Toros weren't so old and serious. If only his mother weren't hanging over us like an enormous buzzard.

Suddenly she swooped into the room. "Are you afraid to perspire? Why don't you scrub harder? Laziness is despised by God."

My back stiffened, and I continued making circular motions with the brush. "Yes, Mother," I said, not even turning to look at her. *"Esh,"* I whispered, the sound blending with the stroke of the bristles over the floor.

Once again Vartanoush sensed my defiance. Her fury was like a windstorm approaching across the desert. She crossed the room quickly and kicked over the bucket, which splashed gray water onto my apron and skirt. Before I could say a word, she grabbed me by the scruff of the neck, as if I were a misbehaving puppy.

"Let go of me! What's the matter with you?" I shouted.

Strength surged through my mother-in-law, and she picked me up, flinging me like a dirty rag onto the frigid back porch, slamming the door. Vartanoush slid the bolt as I yelled and banged on the door. I pulled furiously on the knob. I kicked the door. She was not going to let me in.

My wet skirt and apron clung icily to my legs. I wasn't going to get frostbite waiting for that toad to unlock the door. The central branches of a tree close to the porch looked sturdy enough to hold my weight, and I thought the snow on the ground would break my fall if I slipped. With determination, I swung my leg over the railing. A sharp-faced squirrel scolded me from a branch above, and a boy on a bicycle called out to me in English as he pedaled by. Ignoring both of them, I gripped the railing, lowered my feet to a fork in the tree, then climbed down to the ground. Lucky for me the side door was unlocked, so I hid in the basement for a while before sneaking up the front stairs in time for lunch.

When Toros arrived at noon, Vartanoush stood at the stove, stirring the soup.

"Good day, Mother!" he addressed her in English. "Now that you are in America, you must learn to speak English," he continued in Armenian.

"I'm too old to learn new ways. I speak Armenian, Turkish, and some Arabic. Here, you'll have to be my interpreter." Vartanoush poured the soup into a tureen.

"Where's my wife?"

"Look on the porch," Vartanoush said darkly.

"The porch?" asked Toros.

I had been listening to all this from the dining room. I materialized in the kitchen, trying not to smile. "What would I be doing out on the porch in this kind of weather?"

Vartanoush's chin fell to her chest, and her eyebrows hit her hairline. I took the soup tureen from the stove. "Let me help you with that, Mother," I said in my sweetest voice.

* * *

The weekend passed smoothly—housework, cooking, a street-car ride to the church on Shawmut Avenue, dinner, and a walk along the Charles River on Sunday afternoon. With Toros around, the water's surface was calm. I said nothing at all, except when directly questioned.

I remembered a story the woman who embroidered with Dalita and me had told us one afternoon. In the old days, in the woman's village, there had been a custom that when a bride entered her mother-in-law's house, the girl was not allowed to talk in the presence of the family. The length of the girl's silence depended upon the goodwill of the mother-in-law, who would eventually grant her permission to speak. This Armenian custom was called "the bride has lost her tongue." Only at night, in the privacy of her marriage bed, could the girl address her husband. I thought adopting this custom for a while might be useful.

In our room at night, I pressed Toros for permission to take an English class at the high school two evenings a week. I finally convinced him of the idea, and the next morning he announced to Vartanoush at breakfast that his wife would be taking English lessons. The old squirrel didn't respond right away. Finally she said, "Toros, it is, after all, up to you. If you don't mind that your wife walks the streets alone after dark, there isn't much I can say. When do these classes start?"

"Tonight," I said. "At seven-thirty, and it's only a ten-minute walk."

Vartanoush shot me an acid glance. Confident that her son would be oblivious of her sarcasm, Vartanoush said, "Well, my dear, you certainly have worked everything out. Don't you worry about leaving your husband alone all evening, without your company?"

"I'm sure, Mother, that he will be pleased to have your undivided attention for a few hours." I looked at her sideways.

The mean bird was shocked that I had met blade with blade. Toros was lost in his newspaper. Suddenly, under the table, I felt a sharp pain in my shin. The she-goat had kicked me.

"Aah!" I gasped.

"What?" asked Toros, glancing up from his paper.

"Nothing," Vartanoush and I chimed in unison.

"You're going to be late, my son, unless you hurry."

Toros laughed in protest. "*Mayrig,* the store is three blocks from here, and I'm the boss." But he rose to go.

Vartanoush helped him on with his coat. As he headed down the back stairs, she closed the door and pushed up the sleeves of her sweater, ready to go after me. But with the broom in hand, I raced down the front steps and was vigorously sweeping the front walk as Vartanoush glared down at me through the window.

At supper that night I didn't mind that Vartanoush had burned the bottom of the bulgur so the charred taste went through all the grain. I had made a trip to Woolworth's in the afternoon, where I'd bought a lined notebook and a pencil.

I amused Toros with the story of my dealings with the clerk. "I had to say 'pencil' five times—I said it just as you told me—before he understood what I meant. But he was a nice person; he didn't laugh, and helped me choose a notebook. After I walked up and down the aisles, I sat at the counter and had a soda."

I saw the telltale flush rising up Vartanoush's neck but her anger couldn't touch me.

After the table was cleared, I washed the dishes in about two minutes and was into my coat and hat in thirty seconds. I paused on the landing, with my ear pressed to the kitchen door.

"*Vay, vay, vay,* what is this world coming to, my son?" Vartanoush clucked.

"What does this mean, *Mayrig?*"

"Can you imagine what your father, may the Lord keep him, would have said had I gone out alone at night? Imagine what people at the church will think."

"She's only going to class, Mother."

"What does a wife need lessons for? Can't you teach her everything she needs? Who knows what sort of riffraff will be there. Did you notice she was wearing her best dress?"

"She wants to look nice for the teacher and the other students. She's proud."

"And you know what the Bible says about pride."

I ran down the steps and out of the house, away from her hateful scheming and the sound of creaking bones.

The class was thrilling. I learned how to say "My name is Zabelle Chahasbanian. What's your name? How are you? I am fine, thank you."

When I burst into the door an hour and a half later, my cheeks were ruddy from the brisk walk and I was bright with life.

"Well, look, Toros, here is our little wanderer come home!" the old witch said.

I pronounced in English, bowing from the waist, "Good evening, sir!" I barely looked at Vartanoush, not wanting to spoil my mood.

The next evening, after I finished with the dishes, I listened by the pantry door for more of her campaign against me.

"Son, I only say these things because I want you to be happy. If you let your wife run wild now in the first days of your marriage, what do you think will happen in a few years? She will be out at night, disgracing the family. Remember from Proverbs: 'She is loud and stubborn; her feet abide not in her house.'"

"Zabelle asked my permission to take this class. She wants to learn English so she can help me in the store."

"I have seen these American women working in stores, and it is shameful. They belong in their homes. Your wife,

Toros, your wife should be at home with your children while you are at the store. Think of the good women you know from church. Do their husbands allow them to go around at night? Are they working in stores as shopgirls, showing all their teeth to strange men?"

She paused for a few seconds, then continued, "You've got to put your foot down. In Proverbs, it says finding a virtuous woman is better than finding rubies. Once you have one, you've got to keep her that way."

"If she worked in the store with me, I don't think there'd be a problem. Or maybe she'll take a job at Ohanessian's shirt factory," Toros said. "We could use the extra money right now."

"Don't they all speak Armenian at Ohanessian's?"

I came into the room at that moment. "What about Ohanessian's? I thought I was going to work in the market with you."

Toros grimaced. "We'll see."

I could feel the walls of my defenses crumbling. But I didn't give up. When we went to bed that night, I recited all the American words I had learned and made him laugh at my funny pronunciation, which he corrected. It felt like something we could do together, learning this language. And I believed he would be able to stand up to her.

Two days later I sat at the dining-room table, bent over my notebook, printing the English alphabet. In comparison with

Armenian letters, they seemed like a starched procession, all angles and straight lines, but satisfying when arrayed on the page. Then I started to copy down the days of the week and the months of the year. While I did this, Vartanoush dusted the dishes in a glassed cabinet in one corner of the room. I think it started to get on her nerves that she was working while I sat in a chair.

"Mother," I said, "I'll help you in a few minutes. I'm almost done." Then I asked, "When is Toros's birthday?"

"In August. The fifth. Why do you ask?"

"Just curious. We're learning the months and days of the week."

"Your own birthday, even the year, you don't know." Vartanoush sounded sympathetic.

I looked up, surprised by her kindness but too engrossed to wonder about it. "It doesn't matter," I said.

"You should choose a day."

"Any day?"

"Sure. You can pick a new birthday."

I thought for a moment. "The first of April. It's a spring day, with blue skies."

Vartanoush sighed. "Listen, Zabelle, you're not going anywhere tonight."

"What do you mean? The class meets tonight."

"No . . . Toros decided he doesn't want you to take that class."

"He didn't say anything to me."

"Well, he changed his mind. Of course, he still wants you to learn the language, but not in a roomful of strangers. He doesn't like the idea of you on the street alone at night."

"It's only a few blocks from here. If he's worried, he can walk with me, he can come and meet me."

Vartanoush's patience snapped. "You selfish girl! You think your husband should work all day to put food in your mouth, and then he should be your servant, accompanying you to class and fetching you home again? Who put such ideas in your head?"

"A walk after dinner would do him good," I said. I heard doors slamming shut on me.

"You wretch! I should have known better than to take someone from the house of that accursed cousin of mine, with her French perfume and European notions. And you! It's good that your mother died, rather than see you behave so disrespectfully!" Vartanoush moved close to me, slicing the air in front of my face with her hand.

"Don't you speak the name of my mother!" I shouted, jumping up from the chair, knocking it over. My mother was an angel—she had stopped eating after the baby died so there would be more food for me. Vartanoush was spiteful and selfish, not fit to wipe the shoes of my mother.

This retort was too much for Vartanoush, and she slapped me across the face. When I instinctively put my arms around my head, the old woman beat me on the arms, the shoulders, the back. "Don't you ever," she said between blows, "don't you ever speak to me in that tone of voice again! It must be the devil who puts such evil in your heart!"

I tore myself away and ran to the bedroom I shared with Toros. I slammed the door behind me, turned the lock, and propped the chair under the doorknob for good measure. If the tallboy hadn't been so heavy, I would have pushed that in front of the door as well. I knew I would learn English one way or another, and I would fill my notebook with English words. I'd have a whole page set aside just for bad names to call my mother-in-law. I was furious that Toros had sided with his mother and didn't have the nerve to tell me himself.

My mother-in-law was like some kind of a horrible *dev* from one of the stories my grandmother had told me when I was a child. Always at the end of those tales, the *dev* had been vanquished, drowned in a well or sealed with a boulder into a dark cavern. Was I going to be stuck with Vartanoush forever?

At dinner that night Vartanoush and I would not look at each other. Toros glanced uneasily back and forth between us. My eyes were red from crying, and Vartanoush's glittered with barely controlled fury. Toros knew his mother had informed me of their decision, but he was such a coward that he couldn't even bring up the canceled lessons.

The three of us ate in silence, the sounds of the forks against the plates interrupted only by requests from Toros for the salt or the butter. The rest of the evening dragged by in sullen silence. Toros read the newspaper, his mother wrote a letter to her priest in Istanbul, and I darned socks with stabs of the needle.

Finally it came time to turn off the lamps and go to bed. Toros and I went into our room, and Vartanoush went to hers.

"She despises me!" I said as soon as the door was shut.

"Keep your voice down," he said. "My mother is concerned for my welfare and yours."

"Am I to live for years like this? With the two of us in this house, one of us might end up dead."

"I would sooner send you away than my mother, who raised me, who sacrificed years of her life for me, who lost everyone but me." His voice was icy.

There was nothing else to say. I lay with my back to Toros, careful that not one scrap of nightgown, not even my least toe, touched him. An old man who loved his mother better than his wife. I should have married the spice dealer; at least his mother was dead. Toros was rigid on his side of the bed, too, and I lay awake until I felt the tension ebb as he fell asleep. Now I knew that I was on my own.

After a few days the battle zone quieted with an unspoken cease-fire. Cold weather kept us in the house, so there was no relief from her malice, and I was saving my strength. She talked to me like I was a servant. I addressed her as little as possible. Toros spent more time with his account books in the evening and left earlier in the morning for the store.

I still had my English book, my notebook, and my pencils. Whenever there was a free moment, I worked like a fury to learn that language. I read the newspaper, the back of cereal boxes, the medicine jars in the bathroom cabinet. Every new word I learned was like a brick in a wall between me and my mother-in-law.

One morning several weeks later, snow fell from a dark sky. I was sweeping the kitchen floor, whisking the dust and dried bits of food off the landing onto the stairs. The old woman slammed a pot she was carrying onto the counter and marched over to me.

"What way to sweep is that, you fool? You have spread dirt all over the stairs and dust onto the banisters." She tried to grab the broom from me, but my grip didn't slacken. We faced each other, Vartanoush looking into my determined face. She jerked the broom one direction, and I pulled in the other direction.

"Let go of that broom, you demon!" cried Vartanoush.

"I won't let you hit me with it, and I'm not letting go."

"Have you no respect? Have you no shame? The devil has his hooks in you, and you're going to burn in hell."

We struggled over the broom, our movements getting broader until we rocked dangerously close to the top step. The old woman pulled hard at the wooden handle, and when I yanked it back with equal force, Vartanoush, on a sudden impulse, let go. I sailed down the stairs, the broom flying with me, and crumpled in a heap at the bottom.

I lay there, the wind knocked out of me, and didn't move. Let her think I was dead. Let her imagine explaining to Toros how she killed his wife. I would look angelic in the casket, and Toros would never be able to forgive himself for not standing up to his mother, Satan's handmaiden herself.

Gripping the rail, Vartanoush hurried down the stairs. As she stood over me, her fear like a sour smell, I finally opened my eyes. I rubbed a spot on my skull where a lump was forming.

With not a thread of doubt in my voice, I said, "If you touch me, I'll kill you."

"You snake!" Vartanoush hissed.

She never laid a hand on me again. But it was a long war we fought, living in our house like enemies in tents pitched side by side.

CHAPTER FIVE

The Birth of Love

(WATERTOWN, 1928)

Of all the button sewers at Ohanessian's Shirt Company, I was the fastest. We were paid by the button, so at the end of the week I had earned almost twice as much as the second fastest girl. The other girls weren't jealous. They liked me, because I joined in the gossip and didn't play up to the boss.

Ohanessian was shaped like a pear, with narrow shoulders sloping down to an enormous belly. His eyebrows were poised on his forehead like bushy insects about to take flight. When he was angry, his bald head turned crimson, and when he shouted, spit flew in all directions. He never yelled at me, though, because I was his best worker.

The seamstresses sat in rows behind their sewing machines in one room, where the shirts were made, and we button sewers sat around a long trestle table in another room, with our needles and thimbles. A boy—his name was Moses Bodjakanian—trundled the shirts from one room to the next, taking them finally to a third room where they were pressed and boxed.

At first glance, there was nothing remarkable about Moses. He was an ordinary boy, about my age, who worked in a shirt factory. Not very handsome, not particularly smart. But when I noticed the way he stared at me, his eyes like two lamps, I looked at him closer.

His square hands were steady when he hoisted a bale of shirts. And his ears were perfectly shaped and fitted to his head. He was amusing, full of jokes and laughter, like a small boy or a clown. But when I spoke, he listened intently, as though I were delivering a biblical prophecy. Most of all, though, I liked the way he responded in his gruff, sweet voice.

In the morning as I left my home—which Vartanoush filled with the bad odor of her moods—I felt life seep back into me with each step I took away from the door. By the time I reached Ohanessian's, I had changed from a drab daughter-in-law into a young, strong woman with shining hair, red lips, and a sheen to my skin. The journey home worked the opposite, so that when I entered the house I was as flat and gray as newsprint.

It got to the point that I could barely stand going home at night and counted the hours until the next morning's tray of buttons was set before me. The weekends were suffocating. Toros wasn't a bad man, and I was beginning to feel a certain fondness for him. He was respectful and often kind. But everything between us was controlled by his mother, who loomed like a giant bird of prey. I longed for the sound of Moses's voice, which was full of life, like a sapling growing in a forest of charred tree stumps.

Our flirtation, if you could call it that, was so subtle that the other workers didn't notice anything. Even if anyone had suspected, we never did anything that could be criticized. We were proper in all respects. If romance was a woman who filled a room with strong perfume, our friendship was a girl who left in her wake a hint of soap and damp hair.

When we were working, the girls told stories and gossiped. My needle darted through the button, anchoring it to cloth, no matter what the talk. I always kept half an ear on the discussion.

"Did you see how fat *Digin* Ohanessian has become?" asked Maral Topalian.

"Her double chin has grown a triple chin," said Seta Barsamian. "She could at least get some bigger dresses."

"All she does is read magazines and eat *pakhlava*." Manoush Agahigian grabbed a handful of buttons from the tray.

"If you had a wealthy husband, would you be skinny?"

"If I had a wealthy husband, would I be sitting here sewing buttons?"

"At least your mother-in-law does the cooking."

"You call that cooking?"

My mind drifted to Moses. He ran his hands through the waves of his thick black hair. His face was unmarked, with a high broad forehead. When he laughed, he tipped up his chin and showed his teeth. The way he walked was a rolling dance over the floorboards.

It was a good thing that none of the girls could read my mind. I tried to be fair to Toros, but on certain days—when Vartanoush had been especially nasty, and Toros had hidden behind his newspaper—my husband's list of positive attributes was pitifully small. He sometimes offered to brush my hair at night. He hung his clothes neatly in the closet. His snoring wasn't so loud. And he was a hardworking man who owned property. Moses earned less than I did.

Still, I would daydream. If I were married to Moses, one Sunday after church—or maybe we'd skip church altogether—we would take a picnic and spread a blanket under a tree in the Boston Public Gardens. Moses's mother would live with his older brother's family, so he and I would have an apartment all to ourselves. Breakfast and dinner I would cook, and we would sit down together, just the two of us. Moses would never read the newspaper at the table, and after dinner we'd sit on the porch, watching the sun go down over our garden.

There I stopped. A husband is a husband, I said to myself. I had one, and it was useless to imagine what kind this other one would make.

"My mother-in-law snores so loud that the neighbors bang on the ceiling with a broom," boasted Maral Topalian.

"Mine doesn't sleep at night. She prowls around the house like a thief."

"My mother-in-law is so modest, she wears her underwear in the bathtub," I said. I had never seen Vartanoush in the bathtub, so this might have been true. In any case, everyone laughed.

Sometime after that, my needle began to feel like it was moving through cardboard rather than cotton. Since my speed was the prod that kept everyone working, when I slowed, the number of finished shirts at the end of each day was noticeably fewer. The big boss came in and shouted what was meant to be encouragement.

"Zabelle, what's your husband going to say when he sees the pay you bring home this week?"

Moses was in the room at this moment. If my needle had been a sword, I would have lopped off Ohanessian's head and thrown it to the rats. I leaned over the shirt in my hands, as Moses left the room behind a mountain of cloth. He and I never talked about Toros or anything to do with my life at home.

I tried and tried, but I couldn't seem to push the needle any faster. My stomach was queasier than it had been on the boat from Constantinople, and I was bone weary. I felt like I was swimming in honey. All I wanted to do was crawl under the table, lie on the wooden floor, and take a long nap. It wasn't until Maral made a comment—pointing her eyebrows in my direction—about how tiring the first months of pregnancy were that I admitted to myself what I already knew.

I decided not to say anything—not to Toros, Vartanoush, or Ohanessian. The fear of leaving my job one day before it was necessary made me work as hard as I could. How would I survive interminable days alone in the house with my mother-in-law? Grabbing a handful of bone buttons, I bowed my head over a shirt.

I carried my secret for several months. I'm sure the other girls knew, but no one said a word. Everything continued as usual, including my friendship with Moses. He had taken to joining the button sewers at midday and sat next to me. I brought an extra apple or pear from the market to give to him. If the girls were looking at us sideways, I didn't notice.

When my energy came back, so did my appetite. At meals Vartanoush watched suspiciously as I filled my plate for a second or third time. Her cooking was tasteless, but I would have eaten mattress ticking to appease my hunger. I carried saltine crackers and raisins with me everyplace, trailing crumbs. I stopped to visit Toros at the market, where I'd pick up a candy bar and a piece of cheese. The baby began to turn inside me, flicking his tail like a little fish. Finally my belly was as round as a cantaloupe, and I didn't think I'd be able to disguise my condition much longer.

It was Vartanoush who, with her usual tact, made the announcement as we sat down to Friday dinner. "Well, Toros," she said, "it looks like there's going to be another mouth to feed."

I paused, my fork frozen in midair. I had been planning to speak to Toros that night. Once again the witch had managed to get herself into the middle of our business.

"What do you mean, *Mayrig?*" asked Toros.

"Son," she said, talking with the patience one might use with a moron, "your wife is going to have a baby."

Toros looked to me for confirmation.

"In September," I answered. I knew I'd have to give notice at Ohanessian's on Monday. Back to the gray world of long days under my mother-in-law the prison warden. I sighed.

Toros smiled, pressing his palms together in thanks. "God is blessing our marriage with this child," he said.

Vartanoush added, "I'll pray for a son."

I thought, Lord, don't let me give the world another daughter-in-law.

"It's time to buy a house," said Toros.

All the girls at Ohanessian's were happy for me. The unmarried ones wished they were married; the childless ones wanted a child. There were a few girls with husbands and children, and they were envious that I would no longer have to work at the factory. Ohanessian was annoyed that he would lose his best worker but put a good face on things. He promised me a farewell bonus. I didn't have the heart to say anything to Moses, but I knew he'd already heard that Friday was my last day.

Moses avoided me all week, and I was miserable. He came in and out of the room, dropping off and fetching shirts, but he didn't stop to say anything. He took his lunch elsewhere.

What did I expect? I was married. I was carrying my husband's child. I was leaving work and wouldn't see Moses again. What could I possibly say to him? What did I want from him?

On Thursday, when he paused to say something to another girl, the room suddenly seemed hotter than I could bear. The air was stuffy, the overhead light too bright. My head clouded, and the next thing I knew I was lying on the floor with one girl fanning me and another patting my hand. I saw Moses by the door, but when I met his eyes, he darted out of the room.

On Friday the girls showered me with handmade baby gifts— blankets, knit booties, three cotton gowns with drawstrings, a soft white sweater with mother-of-pearl buttons, and two small bonnets trimmed with satin. It was hard for me to imagine a creature tiny enough to wear these clothes. When Ohanessian handed out the weekly pay, mine included an extra five dollars in a separate envelope. At the end of the day I lingered, not wanting to say farewell to my friends. I wished that Moses would at least say good-bye, but he had disappeared. I left the girls clustered outside the factory's front door and heard their chatter recede as I walked slowly away.

Halfway up Spruce Street—the hill seemed longer and steeper than usual—I sat down on a flight of stone steps in front of a large gray house. Home was close, but I didn't want to go home. I felt the fluttering limbs of the baby as it turned in my belly.

The child inside me had started out as a tiny seed, barely an idea. Already the whorls of his fingerprints had formed, and his ears were listening to the sounds of my rushing blood. He would emerge from my body into the light as a new person, where life would unroll before him like a carpet. An American life.

I glanced up and saw Moses standing a few feet away, half-hidden behind a tree. He walked over to me. I moved to one side on the step, so he could sit down. The six inches between us hummed.

"I'm going to Worcester to work in my mother's cousin's wire factory," he said.

I couldn't even think of anything to say. Each turn of my mind took me down a blind alley.

"I have something for you," he said. "Put out your hand."

Moses extended his closed hand, and I put out my palm, into which he dropped a silver thimble patterned with flowers and tendrils. The silver was warm in my hand.

"It belonged to my grandmother. I kept it knotted in my belt during the deportations."

I felt tears filling my eyes. "I can't take this. It's all you have."

"I have her ring as well."

The ring was for some other girl. I would keep the thimble. "Thank you," I said.

He stood to go. "May the light be with you always."

"And with you," I murmured. I wanted to give him something, but what did I have to give? My dented tin cup? The mirror from my Turkish mistress? The Bible from the Patriarch?

"Moses," I called after him. He turned toward me, his face filled with sadness. I approached with my hand extended. He grasped it, and we shook in the American style. It was an aching relief to feel his warmth and the solid bones under his skin. We should not have touched at all, because this brief meeting of bodies filled me with longing for what I couldn't have.

I pulled my hand back. I said, "I wish you good fortune in all you do. . . ." He bowed his head slightly and continued on his way.

I couldn't help but wonder if I would have been happy with him. What if I had met him first? What if I had been an early widow? What if he had asked me to run away with him and go to Worcester, which seemed half a world away? It did me no good to think like that. I was married to my life by the baby inside me, by my sense of what was right, by my feeling of gratitude to Toros, who had after all given me a home and a family that was mine. Never mind that his mother was a circling buzzard. I was young and foolish enough to believe she couldn't live very long.

That night I handed Toros my pay envelope, as I had each week, and the bonus envelope as well. He took one look at the five-dollar bill and returned it to me.

"Keep this. Use it to buy what you want for the baby, or for yourself."

For Toros, this generosity was an act of love. I slid the note into my pocketbook. Also in my pocketbook, knotted in a handkerchief, was the thimble. The five dollars, which was more money than I'd ever had before, should have made me feel like a wealthy woman.

There was the baby to think of. I would buy white satin to make a small jacket. And I'd sew a matching bonnet, with a ruffle. The stitches would be finer than an eyelash.

Toros bought a two-family house on Walnut Street, on a double lot that fronted on Lincoln Street as well. It was one block from his market. He rented the first-floor apartment to the Kalajian brothers, who worked at the B. F. Goodrich Factory down by the river. Vartanoush did most of the packing and unpacking for the move, with lots of loud grumbling.

Finally, I would have my garden. The people who had lived there before us had spent a great deal of time and care in the yard. Red roses grew over a trellis at the bottom of the walk, and at the top of the walk, pink roses climbed over an arched gate. There were two kinds of pear, a peach tree, and a rose of Sharon bush. The annual beds and the vegetable plot were left fallow that year, because the house had been for sale. My first day in the garden, I sat on a low border wall, yanking up weeds in the herb plot. The sight of dirt under my fingernails made me happy.

There was a grapevine growing up the back of the house and over the back porch. We had missed the season for picking grape leaves to stuff and cook, but I pulled off a few of the vine's small green tendrils, which were crisp and sour. Soon the grapes would ripen, with purple skins and sweet flesh.

In the morning, when Toros headed down the block to the store, I went to the garden. Carrying a child had temporarily exempted me from Vartanoush's scolding. She had no interest in the yard, so I was free of her as long as I stayed out of the house. In the August heat, the end of pregnancy was a drug that made time flow like syrup. After the sidewalk and the marble stepping-stones were swept, I rested in a wicker chair under the pear tree. I read the newspaper, to sharpen my English, but I couldn't concentrate. I watched the passing clouds, and waited. A car drove by. A dog barked. I shut my eyes and drifted back to my early days in Hadjin.

My mother sang in the garden as she hung the freshly washed clothes. A voice said, "Button, button, who's got the button?" My grandmother, my two cousins—Shushan and Anoush—and I held on to the red yarn and passed the white button from under one fist to the next. Who hid the button in her hand?

Occasionally Moses's face flitted across my mind's eye, but his life in Worcester was remote and unimaginable. Most likely he had forgotten me already. Maybe he was married. I kept a small room for him in the house of memory, but as the months passed, he seemed like someone I had invented in my loneliness.

I couldn't keep myself from resting my hands on my enormous belly. The baby rotated like a planet on its axis. He kicked so hard, my dress jumped. He elbowed my ribs and pushed up against my lungs. There seemed to be barely enough room in my body for the both of us. I was afraid of the pain, but more than anything I wanted the baby out of me.

My mother-in-law fussed over me more with each passing day. Don't touch that laundry basket. Have another *lahmejun*. Why don't you go lie down, honey. Maybe I should have been flattered and enjoyed the pampering. Instead I felt like a calf being fattened for the slaughter.

I sensed something change between me, my husband, and my mother-in-law. It was not a leap, but several small steps. Toros made a stool for me to put my feet on in the evening. He brought fresh halvah. One time when the three of us were sitting together on the porch, he briefly put his hand over mine.

When we moved into the new house, Toros and I took the large bedroom on the second floor. The room across the hall was reserved for the baby. Vartanoush had her pick of the three bedrooms under the eaves on the third floor. She knew she had been banished to a distant colony.

In the last weeks before the baby was due, the heat was unbearable. I slept alone on a daybed on the screened front porch. I lay on my side, staring out at the tall pines that framed the house, trying to imagine the baby's face. I wanted him to look like me so that it would be clear that he was mine. I was worried that Vartanoush would claim the baby the minute he emerged.

In early September, one morning toward dawn, I woke up with pains. I lay on the daybed, watching light filter through the trees, as the pains gripped me every so often. When the spaces between them grew shorter, I went to find Toros. He raced to the midwife's house and left me with Vartanoush. I sat in the armchair in our bedroom, shut my eyes, and pretended that my mother-in-law was a buzzing fly bumping against the ceiling.

By the time Toros arrived with the midwife, the contractions felt like I was being squeezed by an enormous fist. The pain pressed all the words out of my body, and I was only pain. In a moment between two contractions, I managed to get across that I wanted Vartanoush out of the room. Toros shepherded her out, over loud protests, and the midwife shut the door.

I climbed a steep mountain peak, where the air was so thin it tore at my lungs. The stones under my feet were sharp and unyielding. There was nothing to do but struggle to the summit. It was unspeakably lonely up there, so far from the town.

The midwife said, "Push," and I did. And I did again.

The boy was small, wrinkled, and red, with a lopsided head and the puffed and folded features of a gnome. What was I supposed to feel for this thing? The midwife cleaned him, wrapped him in a blanket, and placed him in my arms. Half human, half animal, the little creature I held latched on to my breast with a strong, insistent mouth. Then he looked into my eyes.

The midwife bundled the afterbirth in newspaper, wound up the bloodied sheets, and called to Vartanoush and Toros. They were beaming when they came into the room.

"What a fine boy!" said the father.

"What will you call him?" asked the old woman of her son.

I answered before Toros, and almost without thinking, "Moses." I paused for a second, knowing that to seal this thing I had to offer an explanation. I said, "He is chosen to be a great leader."

What could Toros or Vartanoush say in the face of biblical prophesy? I rubbed my cheek against the baby's soft, tawny hair. It was a secret baptism. Now he was mine.

CHAPTER SIX

Ways of the Wicked

(BOSTON, 1931)

The first weeks after Moses was born, everything was pared away, leaving only me and the baby. I slept when he slept, losing track of whether it was day or night. I knew he was hungry before he cried, because the milk let down, spreading wet circles on my dressing gown. My clothes smelled of sour milk and spit-up, my hair was always coming undone, and there were purple circles around my eyes. But I didn't care. Holding his tiny foot in my palm while he gazed up at me was my greatest pleasure.

Mewing kitten, squealing piglet, bleating kid, a barnyard nursery in the bassinet next to our bed. When he cried, he opened his throat and let out ear-splitting yowls. Poor Toros, who worked long hours at the market, groaned and shifted in the bed, pulling a pillow over his head. Soon I moved Moses into his room across the hall, where the two of us slept on a single bed. Sometimes, in the blur between wake and sleep, drunk with the warmth, softness, and sweet smell of the baby, I felt myself cradled in my mother's arms.

Eventually Moses slept in his crib and I returned to the double bed I shared with Toros. Sometimes my husband and I stood together, admiring our sleeping baby, who, to us, was the most beautiful boy in the world. For a few moments, this singular child was a wooden bridge linking two banks of a river.

Other things changed as well. I no longer felt that Vartanoush was perched on our headboard like a glassy-eyed crow. She found room in her flinty heart for little Moses. She bathed him in the kitchen sink, not complaining when he splashed water on her dress. She took him into her lap and whispered into his ear. Vartanoush and I were never friends, but Moses softened the air between us.

Soon the boy was walking, then chasing the neighbor's cat up and down the yard, calling, *"Gadu, gadu."* He followed me around the garden and the house, watching everything I did with big eyes. He was neat and precise, even as a toddler, insisting on changing his clothes if they were the least bit soiled. My little old man, I called him.

One Sunday when we rode the streetcar to the Armenian church on Shawmut Avenue in Boston, Moses, who was almost three, sat in my lap, looking out the window. I saw myself in the glass, holding a solemn, fair-haired child. Toros was next to me in his Sunday best, his black-clad mother across from us. This is my family, I said to myself.

We arrived early, which was the Chahasbanian way, and so had our choice of pews. Toros liked to be a little more than halfway back, on the left side and on the aisle. Minutes after we were seated, Moses and Vartanoush closed their eyes and slept through the liturgy and the prayers.

Toward the end of the service, out of the corner of my eye I noticed a woman across the aisle, waving to me. I turned to look at her. She had a heart-shaped face, framed by black hair under an emerald hat. Gesturing toward the door, she mouthed, "Outside." She wanted me to join her in the vestibule. Without thinking, I followed her up the aisle and out of the sanctuary.

"Zabelle, honey, don't you recognize me?" the woman asked.

Before my eyes flashed Arsinee and Sarkis waving goodbye to me on the day they left the orphanage. Then Arsinee giving Sarkis water from my tin cup. Our three sets of dirty feet in the sand. Black tents.

When I opened my eyes, my head was in Arsinee's lap as she fanned me with a lace-edged handkerchief.

"I don't know how you got along without me," Arsinee said.

"I don't either," I said.

She wiped the tears from my eyes with her handkerchief.

"How long has it been?" she asked.

"A hundred years," I said. "The last time I saw you, you were as thin as a stick, with a head full of lice."

"Those were the days," Arsinee said with a sigh. And we both laughed.

The doors opened as the service ended, and we scrambled to our feet. We were swept along in a sea of people out into the sunny street. Toros, Moses, and Vartanoush made their way to us through the buzzing crowd. I introduced them to Arsinee, except I didn't know her last name.

"Manoogian," she said. "And here comes my husband."

"Manoogian," Toros muttered under his breath. "First time he's been to church in years."

"Chahasbanian! How's business?" said Arsinee's husband. He was about the same age as Toros. Handsome, tall, with a fine suit and a mustache that curled neatly at the corners of his mouth. The thin old man at his elbow looked like a ghostly version of his son, all gray and shadows.

My husband shrugged. "People have to eat. How about you?"

"People need clothes on their backs," Manoogian replied.

I could tell the men didn't like each other. They were two dogs, circling each other with bared teeth and bristling hair.

Arsinee's mother-in-law was round and squat like a tree stump, with dark hair on her arms and small mean eyes. She had Arsinee's baby with her. Henry, who was about the same age as Moses, looked like he had dropped from his father's nostril, as we say.

Manoogian tapped on the face of his gold watch. "Alice, I think it's time we were going."

Arsinee gave me a hug and whispered in my ear, "Don't call me that *odar* name. My husband thinks Alice makes me more American."

"When can I come visit?" she said in a louder voice.

I glanced at the frowning face of my mother-in-law. Then I looked at Arsinee's mother-in-law, who could have been Vartanoush's uglier twin.

Arsinee suggested, "Why don't we meet at the school park on Wednesday afternoon. Around three."

For me, finding Arsinee was like Jesus raising Lazarus from the tomb. When she left the orphanage, my last link to my childhood in Hadjin was gone. I was sure that she and Sarkis had died on the road to Mersin. Years later and thousands of miles away, she bloomed like a forgotten bulb in the garden. A scarlet tulip among the daffodils. I hadn't known what I was missing until it was returned to me. Nothing—husbands, mothers-in-law, acts of war, natural disasters—would ever separate Arsinee and me again.

After dinner that afternoon, as we were washing the dishes, Vartanoush started needling me about Arsinee. It was predictable. She couldn't stand the scent of my happiness.

"How do you know that Manoogian girl?"

"She comes from the same town as my family." I tucked the dish towel into the waistband of my apron and carried a stack of dishes into the pantry. I made a sour face at the shelves.

"I'm not sure I like her," Vartanoush continued. "Did you notice how short her skirt was? It barely came to her knees, and stuck to her like her own skin."

"It was almost to her ankles." I looked through narrowed eyes at my mother-in-law's shapeless black dress and lint-covered black sweater. She had a bunched-up, graying handkerchief dangling out of the sleeve.

"Hmmph. Alice." Vartanoush pursed her lips. "Some name for an Armenian girl. Her husband seems to think he's a big shot just because he owns a clothes store. And that girl's red cheeks aren't from nature."

I watched the old woman's nose twitch above her faint white mustache and downturned mouth. She had never looked more like a rat. "Her name's Arsinee."

"You told her you'd meet her at the park? What kind of place is that to meet someone? There's all types of riffraff on the streets these days. Are you embarrassed of your own home? What if she doesn't come right away, and you're sitting there all alone in the park? How will that look? Who's going to watch Moses while you're out?"

"I'll take him with me," I said.

"Of course not. I'll watch my little angel."

Moses was my shadow in the garden and the house. I had wanted a few hours of freedom, which her jealousy would buy me.

In the late afternoon that same day, the Melkonians, a young couple who had recently arrived from Aleppo, came by for coffee. Moses played under the dining room table with a little wooden train Toros had bought him. I set a plate of *cheoregs* I had made on the table, along with some string cheese and homemade pear jelly. Vartanoush carried in a tray of Turkish coffee and tea.

It was Toros's habit to read the Sunday paper from one end to the other. Then he would recount the most depressing items, with commentary. It brought out the Protestant in him, so we were treated to a second sermon. That day, he finished the catalog of ruin and disaster with a lecture on the financial and spiritual bankruptcy of the whole country—the corruption of politicians, the evil of bootleggers, the squandered lives of drinkers, and the sinful ways of Hollywood movie stars.

"Shameless, godless creatures, I tell you. They swim in diamonds and furs while around them people are starving. And the lives they lead! How many marriages? How many children out of wedlock? The goings-on in that wretched town are too scandalous to mention before our good women."

Vartanoush murmured her approval. The Melkonians nodded in assent. I spread my hands on the table to examine my nails, which needed filing. It occurred to me that I might join Moses under the table to play with the train. My husband was a good father, with fine qualities, but his righteous diatribes annoyed me. He should have been a preacher or a politician, instead of wasting all that breath on us. But the Melkonians and Vartanoush seemed to appreciate his words.

He went on, "Every God-fearing Christian man who goes to see these movies is giving his hard-earned money to support sinners in their wicked, wicked ways."

"Not to mention," added Vartanoush, "that he is filling his head with thoughts unworthy of a good Christian."

Varsenic Melkonian said, "When Hagop and I were walking the other day, I saw a picture of an actress in front of the Coolidge Theatre. She was half-naked, and I had to look the other way."

"I told my wife to turn her face," Hagop Melkonian boasted. "The movie was called *The Tarnished Lady.*"

I imagined Hagop's tongue lolling out of his mouth as he stared at the half-naked woman, while his wife, following his orders, covered her eyes with pudgy hands and walked right into a street sign.

"Shameless," interjected Vartanoush.

"That's Tallulah Bankhead," I said. What a wonderful name that woman had. It rolled on the tongue like a grape. At that moment, I was ready to take the next bus to join her in Hollywood.

Everyone turned to look at me. Moses came out from under the table, and I lifted him into my lap. I closed my eyes and rested my cheek on the top of his head. He was growing as fast as a vine.

Toros continued, "I see the names of the movies in the paper. *Transgression. Laughing Sinners.* They won't be laughing so hard on Judgment Day."

On Wednesday afternoon I put on my best clothes, as though I were going to meet the president's wife. Vartanoush had to get in a few snippy parting remarks. But I wasn't going to let her bother me.

"What are you all dressed up for?"

"I feel like it."

"Pride goeth before the fall."

I didn't say, "The mouth of a fool poureth out foolishness." I had started memorizing verses from my English Bible. I recited them in my head in response to Vartanoush. I could have said them out loud if I wanted, because she never learned more than three words of English.

As I headed down the stairs, I said, "If he's not up in an hour, you should wake him."

"You act like I don't know my own grandson," she called after me.

As soon as I was out the back gate, I felt like I had shed

a heavy coat with stones in its pockets. My shoes skimmed the sidewalk. I passed the market on Mount Auburn Street, where Toros was at the cash register, giving change to a customer. He didn't notice me go by. It was as if I were invisible or another person altogether.

When I reached the park, I saw Arsinee coming across the open field. We both started running and met in the middle, breathless and happy. I felt young, not like an old married woman.

"Come on," said Arsinee, taking my arm, "let's sit under the trees."

"Not on the bench?" I didn't want to ruin my best dress.

"It's nicer over there in the shade."

Out of a carpetbag, Arsinee pulled a tablecloth. "I brought this for us to sit on. My mother-in-law will take the rug beater to me if she finds out, but there's no reason she should know."

"She beats you?" I shouldn't have been surprised, but it made me angry.

"When she gets a chance. The old demon has a temper, but I stay out of trouble. Most of the time."

"What does your husband say?"

Arsinee laughed broadly, showing the gold crowns of her teeth. "He's happy to let her keep me in line."

Nobody did any hitting in our house anymore. Once in a while Moses got a swat on the seat of his pants, but that was it. Toros was the kind of man who shouted and banged doors. When he was truly furious, he glowered like a volcano. But no beating. Not even from Vartanoush, not since that time she knocked me down the stairs.

"Zabelle, don't make big eyes. She hasn't hit me in months. And Peter brings me a new dress whenever she does. What about your mother-in-law? Now that's a mean-looking weasel. And how old's your husband, anyway?"

"Almost forty. He's like an old man—he never wants to go out."

"And I thought my husband was over-the-hill. Peter is thirty-five. We're too young to be stuck with such old goats."

"Toros is a good man," I said. "And his mother does a lot of the housework." I didn't mention that she still did most of the cooking and that the food tasted like shoe leather.

"You're so soft, Zabelle. If I hadn't found food for us, you would have starved. 'Oh no, Arsinee, I can't beg for money! Oh, Arsinee, I can't eat that!' I made you do it. I had to be *jarbig* for the three of us."

"If I hadn't said no, we'd have been eating boiled bits of rag."

"And would it have killed you?"

"No, but eating that lard the woman threw in the alley almost did."

"So I made one mistake. But if it weren't for me, you would have been another pile of bones rotting in the sun."

I didn't say anything.

"You, me, and Sarkis, we did okay," she said.

"What happened to Sarkis?" I asked.

"When I left for America, he was still with the uncle in Mersin. He's in Cairo now. I got a letter last month. What about you? What happened after we left?"

I told her about the Aziz, the Der Stepanians, and Vartanoush Chahasbanian's bringing me to Boston. She explained how Peter Manoogian came to Mersin, where his family was from, to find a wife.

"His mother told him to go to the old country, to find an old country girl. There were orphans every place, all you had to do was choose. He took one look at me in my uncle's café, and decided I was the one for him. It's a good thing his parents were already in America, because his bulldog of a mother would never have approved. She thinks a daughter-in-law should be a kitchen maid, silent as a cooking pot. You can imagine how well she likes my talk."

I laughed. "At least in my case, Vartanoush could blame only herself."

"Listen," proposed Arsinee, "let's not talk about the past anymore. We have our lives here. We have our babies. What's done is done."

"I still think about the deportations. I have terrible dreams. But I never say anything."

"Let's make a pact not to talk about it until we're toothless grandmothers. Then if we want to, we can babble, weep into our aprons, and drive our daughters-in-law crazy."

* * *

Vartanoush didn't care for Arsinee, and Arsinee's mother-in-law liked me less. It was hard for us to see each other as often as we wanted. At that time there was no phone at our house, so I had to go down to the store to call Arsinee.

Every couple of weeks Arsinee and Henry came over for an afternoon. We sat in the garden, where the zinnias, petunias, and pansies were in bloom. Toros's tomato plants were two feet high. Henry and Moses turned up the marble stepping-stones in the lawn to play with the bugs underneath. This kept them occupied for hours. Arsinee wore fine dresses with stockings. So she sat in the wicker chair, telling jokes while I pulled weeds from the beds.

"Let's take the streetcar to Boston," Arsinee said.

"What for?"

"To go to the cinema." Arsinee grinned and lifted one eyebrow. "When I was in town with Peter, I saw a poster for a moving picture we could see."

"We can't go to the cinema!" Toros would bluster and rage if he found out. He would forbid me to see Arsinee—he thought she was a bad influence already. Vartanoush would cluck her tongue for weeks.

"The picture is made by an Armenian. Rouben Mamoulian. How bad could it be?"

"He's probably not a Christian."

"What do you think, he's a Mohammedan?"

"No," I said doubtfully. "But, I don't have the money."

"It's not so expensive, and I'll pay."

"I don't know."

"Have you ever been inside a cinema?" Arsinee already knew the answer.

"No." I turned the idea over like a coin in my hand. It was exciting. But like a schoolgirl, I was afraid we'd get caught.

"I can tell you want to."

"But Toros . . ."

"He doesn't have to know. Do you want to go to your grave without having been?"

"What will we say?"

"We'll say we're going into Boston on the streetcar to buy some . . ."

"To get some thread, and a zipper," I said. "It's true, you know. I do need a zipper, thread, and buttons for the dress I'm making. We wouldn't have to lie. We could say we were going to the Windsor Button Shop."

"Or to Filene's Bargain Basement. We'll take in a Friday matinee."

My life was a dull gray dress, and Arsinee arrived bringing rhinestone buttons and a black velvet collar. Who could resist her?

The first thing we did in Boston was buy a zipper, a card of royal blue buttons, and two spools of matching thread. Then we went to the movie theater, with its big marquee and tall bright posters. On one of the posters, a young girl, dressed modestly in white, stood torn between her burlesque queen mother and a handsome, respectable young man. The mother was half-naked. I tipped my head to one side and looked at Arsinee.

"Directed by Rouben Mamoulian." Arsinee pointed.

"Arsinee," I hissed, "look at the way that woman is dressed." I was afraid someone from the church would be passing by and spot us.

"You've never seen a nightgown?"

"I wouldn't exactly call that a nightgown," I responded. I pointed my eyes in the direction of the theater entrance, where a steady stream of men flowed in. "I've counted two women going in, and they were with men."

"Are you telling me that we came all the way here, that I bought these"—here Arsinee brandished two tickets—"and you're afraid to go in because some *odar* men are in there?"

I didn't say anything.

"Well, I'm going, with or without you." Arsinee marched forward.

"You can't go in there alone!" I hurried behind her through the bright lobby into the darkened theater. A newsreel flickered on the screen as we stumbled down the aisle. Big as life, Al Capone, surrounded by his bodyguards, waved at me. He was mobbed by cheering fans who clamored for autographs. The gangster was a movie star.

We slid into seats, Arsinee on the aisle and me next to

her. Suddenly I was seized with panic. We were in a dark room surrounded by strange men. My husband would never believe it of me. My mother-in-law would curse me. The police were going to arrest us. God was going to strike me down in my seat.

I said to Arsinee, "It's dark in here. I have a bad feeling. Why does it have to be so dark?"

"What's the matter with you? Once in your life will you be brave? Are you going to go through your life whining and wringing your hands? You should be happy to be alive. You should be pleased to see new things."

A man behind us leaned forward, tapping me on the shoulder, which caused both of us to jump. He said in English, "Excuse me, girls, would you mind piping down so I can hear the newsreel?"

Arsinee glared at him, and we turned toward the screen. A long column of bedraggled men waited for dinner in a breadline. Some of them stared into the audience, their eyes vacant or filled with shame. The camera scrolled past park benches, where men and even women wrapped in newspapers and rags lay sleeping. We had passed scenes like that on the street. On the screen they were glamorous and tragic, instead of threadbare and dirty.

"Meanwhile, in Hollywood," the narrator blared. A party: bare-shouldered women, with jewels, danced with tall thin men in tuxedoes and sleek dark heads. They laughed at unheard jokes and winked at the audience.

I muttered under my breath, "Wicked, wicked ways."

Arsinee whispered loudly, "You sound like your mother-in-law. Next you'll be twitching your nose, and wagging your head. Then your face will harden into stone, and they'll bury you in that garden you love so much."

The man behind us sighed loudly.

The feature came on the screen. The mother's clothes were skimpy, her work was degrading, and her husband was a nasty man. But she had a good heart all the same. She adored her beautiful, innocent daughter and wanted to make sure the girl had a comfortable life. Who could blame her?

By the middle of the film I could have wrung out my handkerchief. Even hardheaded Arsinee was sniffling beside me. How could the mother let her evil husband force the lovely daughter into the burlesque theater? The poor girl danced on the stage in her underwear. She and her mother needed money, and the mother wasn't young anymore. Would the daughter's rich boyfriend find out? Could he save the girl, or would he abandon her to her fate?

Suddenly a lewd white face appeared in front of me. It was as if someone had dowsed me with a bucket of cold water, rousing me from a vivid dream. A clean-shaven man with red hair and beady eyes seated directly in front of us had turned around in his seat. He winked at me with a sneer. Arsinee, still absorbed in the film, didn't notice what was going on. I tried to ignore him, but then he whispered something at me. The words were unclear, but the tone was foul and insulting.

I elbowed Arsinee, who said, "What's the matter with you?"

"That man . . ."

"What man?" Arsinee reluctantly pulled her gaze from the screen and saw the leering man. Just then he vaulted over the seat and sat down next to me. I leaped up. Arsinee jumped out of her seat, and the two of us scurried out of the theater. As we reached the exit, Arsinee glanced back and saw that the man was following us.

We raced out into the street. I stumbled into an apple peddler on the sidewalk, upturning his crate of fruit, which rolled around my feet. The peddler cursed, but before I could apologize, Arsinee had grabbed my hand and started to run. The red-haired *dev* was after us like a hound. I lost my hat, and my hair flew in all directions. We darted through the pedestrians and gained a safe distance from the man. He had slowed his pace but was still coming.

Arsinee stopped abruptly. She was furious. "That red-headed *odar*, some stupid *esh*, isn't going to scare me. I'll stick him with my hatpin, and kick him in the shins."

I pleaded, "Don't do that! Look, he's still coming." A streetcar stopped on the curb in front of us, and I dragged Arsinee inside. The man reached the corner just as the doors snapped shut. He laughed and waved as the streetcar pulled away.

We collapsed into seats.

"Look, look what happened because we sinned. I told you something bad was going to happen." I started crying.

"Oh, my God, what a baby you are. If you're going to be like this, I'm getting off right now. Is it our fault that some crazy *odar* chases us out of the theater? I'm so mad. Now we'll never know the end of the story. If I ever see that man again, I'll kick him in the pants. We should have called the police, that's what we should have done. We should have told the theater manager. But no, we run like two headless hens. It's enough to make me ill." She slumped back in the seat.

We sat in silence for a few minutes. I peered into the torn paper sack in my lap. The buttons and the zipper were gone. One spool of blue thread remained. I gazed out the window at an unfamiliar street. I asked, "Do we know where this street-car is going?"

We ended up in Newton Corner, where we had to catch another streetcar to Watertown. It took us an extra hour to get home. Arsinee helped fix my hair and spent the rest of the time haranguing me. She didn't want Toros to know what happened.

"Do you want to be banished from each other? Do you want my mother-in-law to chase me around the house with the rug beater? Be reasonable, Zabelle. What happened wasn't our fault. And besides, we'll never do it again. That was it, the one and only trip to the moving pictures."

By the time we parted at the Walnut Street stop, I had decided not to tell. But walking up the front stairs, I started to feel miserable again.

"So, stranger, funny to see you here," Vartanoush remarked sarcastically. "Did you fall into the Charles River? Where's your hat?"

I burst into tears and dropped into a chair at the kitchen table, with my face in my hands.

"*Yavrum*, what's the matter? Did something happen?" she asked.

At this sign of sympathy from my mother-in-law, a wave of guilt crashed over me. I cried harder.

"Toros! Toros! *Aman im!* Something's the matter with Zabelle!"

Toros entered the kitchen carrying Moses, who started whimpering when he saw me. Toros put the child down, and Moses ran to me. I gathered him into my lap. Toros laid a hand on my shoulder.

"What happened? Tell me, Zabelle," he said firmly.

The pause between his question and my answer was a few seconds. In that time, the afternoon played in fast motion on the screen in my head. They would never understand. I had to be loyal to Arsinee.

I looked up through bleary eyes and said, "I lost the buttons I bought, but I still have the thread. Then we got on the wrong streetcar and ended up in Brookline, and we could only get a streetcar to Newton Corner. Arsinee twisted her ankle getting down the steps, so she couldn't walk very well. We waited for the longest time for a streetcar to Watertown Square, and then another one up Mount Auburn Street. We spent the whole day traveling, and I don't even have the buttons for my dress."

Vartanoush said, "Well, it's nothing to be so upset about."

"I guess you're right," I said, forcing a smile.

The words had spilled out of me as though thread were unwinding from a spool speeding across the floor. And they believed me.

CHAPTER SEVEN

Other Lives

(WORCESTER, 1937)

Children are like seeds: the amount of water and sun and type of soil can influence how tall or broad a plant becomes, but the shape of leaf and color of petal is determined before the sprout breaks through the earth. When Moses was seven, our second son was born, and Toros called him Jack, a tough American name that suited our boy. From the minute he could crawl, Jack headed for trouble like a homing pigeon. Electrical outlets and butter knives were his toys of choice. When he was eleven months old, and on the verge of walking, I gave birth to a daughter whom we named Joy. In daylight hours, she was a placid baby, happily playing with a set of measuring spoons, but every night her stubborn wails dragged me from my bed. Some nights, she screamed as though her crib were a vat of boiling oil.

Between caring for the two babies, I barely had an hour's rest. With cracked and chapped hands, I spent hours of my day changing, rinsing, and wringing diapers. Gone were the long conversations Moses and I had shared while puttering around the garden. With Jack and Joy to compare him to, I realized what an easy child Moses had been.

Good Friday morning, in a rare moment of peace, Arsinee and I drank coffee at the dining-room table, while our children played in the living room. The baby was down for a nap. Arsinee's second child, Dahlia, had wrapped herself in a shawl and stood on the hassock, pretending to be the goddess of love and beauty.

"Bow down before your queen!" she commanded Henry and Moses.

Seated on the rug, the boys were making paper airplanes out of newspaper. They ignored Dahlia. She climbed down and sashayed off to the bathroom. Arsinee and I laughed into our cuffs.

"It's a good thing Vartanoush isn't here," I said. "Pagan goddesses aren't her cup of tea."

"Where is she?" asked Arsinee.

"She and Toros went to get gas for the car. After lunch, we drive to Worcester."

"You won't be in church?"

"We're visiting Toros's friend the clock fixer from Adana. I've never met him before. Toros says the church in Worcester is nice."

Arsinee asked, "Where's Jack?"

"Under the table." I lifted the lace tablecloth and peered in. No Jack. I ran to the living room, and there he was, tearing strips of wallpaper from behind the couch. Kneeling down, I squeezed Jack's jaw open and extracted a wadded mass of paper.

"No, no, no!" I said to Jack, lifting him up.

He shook his head back and forth, then gave me his most charming smile.

"Moses," I said, "did you see what your brother was doing?"

"Sorry, Ma. I thought he was with you," Moses replied.

When Toros and Vartanoush arrived home, he presented me with two sacks of half-rotten fruit and vegetables, as he often did at week's end. But I had no patience for it that day. The suitcase wasn't packed, and the shredded blanket Jack required at bedtime was missing. I was too busy to deal with this rubbish Toros brought home from the store.

When I pointed out that most of it was beyond salvage, Toros said, "In the old country, we ate cats and dogs, we were so hungry. This food is good enough for Roosevelt." I imagined shouting, "Then why don't you give it to Roosevelt's wife?" Instead I hefted the bags to the back porch for sorting, where I tossed most of it into the forsythia bushes.

Before we left, I called Arsinee on the telephone, our new luxury, to tell her good-bye. Out in the driveway, Toros leaned on the car horn.

"It's not like he's dragging you to prison," Arsinee said.

"How would you like to be cooped up in a box on wheels with three whining children and Vartanoush singing bits of the Divine Liturgy?"

Vartanoush sat beside Toros in the front seat, humming "Christ Is Risen" off-key. The motor rumbled, and a noisy draft of cold air shot in the windows. Toros insisted on what he called "fresh air," but I was freezing. I had a scarf over my hair, a coat buttoned to the neck, and a blanket over my lap. The children were bundled in their winter coats.

The baby snuggled on one side of my lap, and Moses was curled up asleep with his head on my other leg. Jack was hunkered down in the deep floor well, playing with blocks. Jack handed Joy a block, and she immediately put it in her mouth. He demanded that she return it, but the baby refused.

"Jack, *yavrum*, you have to share," I told him.

He screeched and threw another block at Joy. It grazed her eyebrow, and she began to shriek, all the while keeping a tight grip on the block he wanted. Jack howled louder. Moses sat up, rubbing his eyes.

Toros shouted from the front seat, "Jack, you hush up or I'm going to pull over and give you a spanking."

Vartanoush twisted her head around, glaring through her bifocals. "How is Toros supposed to drive with all this racket?"

I thought I might shrivel up and die from exhaustion, and then the babies would be orphans with only Toros and Vartanoush to look after them. They'd lock Joy in the closet at night and tie Jack to a chair during the day. Moses would come to put roses on my grave. Poor Moses. Who would check that he washed behind his ears? Who would choose his clothes for school each morning?

I closed my eyes. A red velvet curtain descended around me. *He makes the storm calm, so that the waves are still. . . . I went down into the valley to see whether the pomegranates had budded. . . . Truly the light is sweet, and a pleasant thing it is for the eyes to behold the sun. . . .*

When I opened my eyes, Jack was asleep on the floor, placid as an angel. The baby sucked her thumb and grasped the coveted block in her other hand. Moses had moved to the far window and sat with his cheek against the glass. Out my window I saw a road sign: "Worcester, 10 miles."

Easter in Worcester. We would miss services at the Saint James in Watertown—the church Toros and Peter Manoogian had helped to found the year before. From the church steps, our *Der Hayr* would release twelve white doves. Probably the priest in Worcester would do the same.

We pulled into the driveway of a white three-decker house. Two women—a round woman with graying hair and a skinny young one with a big nose—hurried onto the front porch, untying their aprons as they came.

The older woman called, "*Baron* Chahasbanian, it's so good to see you!"

Toros shook her hand vigorously. "Aghavni, don't be so formal! Hello, Anahit!" He shook the young woman's hand.

"You look more like your father than ever. Except you have your mother's velvet eyes."

I glanced at Toros out of the side of my eyes. I had never heard him be so poetic.

"This is my mother, Vartanoush. My wife, Zabelle, the children, Moses, Jack, and Joy, in order of appearance."

The two women laughed.

Since when did Toros make jokes?

The smell of simmering onions had made its way to the dark entrance hall, where we hung our coats. Oriental rugs covered the floors of the front room. The overstuffed furniture was upholstered in plush, wine-colored fabric. Theirs wasn't so different from our house, except for the clocks. A cuckoo clock hung on the wall, a gold clock gleamed under a crystal dome, there was a massive grandfather clock in the hall. In all, I counted fourteen clocks. The ticking, ringing, and gonging made me nervous.

We climbed to the second-floor apartment with skinny Anahit, who lived there with her husband. Anahit and her husband had a crib in their second bedroom, plus a double bed and a cot. Vartanoush, Jack, the baby, and I would stay there. Toros and Moses would sleep in the spare bedroom on the first floor.

Aghavni wouldn't allow us to help in the kitchen, so we waited in the living room. Toros read his paper, Vartanoush opened her Bible, and Moses kneeled at the coffee table, writing sums with a thick yellow pencil. I sat with Joy and Jack, who attempted to roll a ball back and forth between them. In the dining room, Anahit added extra leaves to the table.

When Boghos Boghosian arrived home from work with his son and son-in-law, I was still on the floor with the babies. I stood to be introduced and suddenly found myself staring into a face from my past. My head began to spin with a kaleidoscope of images—*Baron* Ohanessian's mustache, hands spread on the wooden table, button, needle, spool of thread. Thimble. I closed my eyes, and when I opened them, I was lying on the carpet staring at a circle of faces above me. Moses Bodjakanian leaned in from behind a man with an enormous nose.

Moses Chahasbanian asked, "Ma, are you okay?"

"I'm fine." I sat up slowly. "I just got up too fast, and all the blood rushed to my head." Toros helped me stand, then I sank to the couch, pulling Joy onto my lap.

I had no idea what to do next. I added up the hours we would spend with the Boghosians and the meals we would sit down to with Moses Bodjakanian and his hawk-nosed wife. Should I pretend I'd never met him before? For a minute I wished I were Arsinee.

Arsinee would say, "Moses and I knew each other years ago at Ohanessian's. I fainted because of the shock of seeing he's lost half his hair." Moses's hairline had climbed so far up his forehead that his head looked like an egg. But I kept my mouth shut.

At the crowded dinner table, the conversation sounded like the twittering of birds. I avoided staring at Moses but couldn't stop myself from examining his wife anew. Anahit had an oversize *dolma* of a nose, which she had inherited from her father. A nose like that on a man could be noble, but on a girl it was a curse. God had scrimped on her mouth, which was the size of a postage stamp. I had to admit she had pretty eyes—large and deep with long, curling lashes—which helped draw attention away from the eggplant anchored between them. If Anahit turned sideways in the wind, that nose would be a sail pushing her down the street.

I forced down a spoonful of soup and some pilaf. Moses was silent, pushing pieces of chicken from one side of his plate to the other.

Vartanoush came up to me after the meal and said, "Don't tell me you're pregnant again."

I wanted to say, "You'll be burying me nine months from now if I am," but I wouldn't give the old woman the satisfaction. Instead I snapped, "I'm tired."

The evening dragged on. The clocks stretched each minute to its limit. The little cuckoo was horribly cheerful. I barely said a word, except to address the children. Twice I felt the heat of Moses's eyes on me, but I didn't glance up.

Finally it was time to put the children to bed. Then I realized I would be sleeping in the room next to Anahit and Moses's bedroom. What choice was there?

Little Moses came upstairs with me and the babies. Anahit handed Vartanoush a stack of towels and showed us the light switch in the bathroom. Moses Bodjakanian disappeared into his bedroom with an almost inaudible "Good night."

Once the door was shut behind them, Vartanoush said, "What's the matter with that girl's husband? He didn't open his mouth all night. Do you think he's an imbecile?"

"Ma," said my Moses, "do I have to sleep downstairs?"

"There's no place for you here, honey," I said.

"There are too many clocks in that room. One of them's in the shape of a polar bear. And Pa snores so loud, it's like sleeping in a room with a motorcycle. Can't I stay in the bed with you and Jack?"

"You're too old to sleep with your mother," growled Vartanoush, who sat in the cot in a white flannel gown. She went back to reading her Bible. Her eyesight was so bad, even with glasses on, she held the book three inches from her face.

"Go on." I pushed him gently toward the door. "I'll come down and tuck you in after the babies are asleep."

Moses bowed his head and slunk out of the room.

I settled Jack with a bottle and his blanket by the wall in the double bed. He fell asleep immediately. I nursed Joy, and after her eyes closed, I put her in the crib. Vartanoush had dozed off. I removed the Bible from her chest, and the glasses from the bridge of her nose, and turned out light.

I slipped out of the room and down the back stairs. When I crossed the first-floor kitchen, I saw my husband and his friend seated in armchairs in the parlor. In the lamp's gold light, they leaned toward each other like conspirators. Toros laughed, throwing his head back, slapping the arm of his chair. I glimpsed him as a man in that moment—not my husband, not my children's father, not a grocer or a church deacon, but someone whose inner workings I could never know.

I found my Moses kneeling on the floor by his bed, his hands clasped.

"I prayed that you would come soon," Moses said.

"Sometimes God answers prayers."

I sat beside him, stroking his hair, as he lay in bed. There were no shadows in his eyes, and his face was smooth as an apricot. My love for this child had roots that spread through my veins and into the capillaries. It moved like blood.

"Tell me a story, Ma."

"What kind? "

"My story."

I began, "Once there was, there was not, there was a boy named Moses. He was a handsome, intelligent boy with blond hair, a strong nose, and two eyes that were meant to see the gates of heaven. One day Moses packed a small suitcase, complete with a lunch his mother had made him, and set off down the street to have an adventure. . . ." That was as far as the adventurer traveled, because Moses had drifted toward dreaming. I thought of an Easter dove, its soft downy body in the priest's hands the moment before flight.

When I opened the door to the darkened second-floor

apartment, the light fell in behind me. Moses Bodjakanian was seated at the kitchen table with his head in his hands.

I stepped inside and shut the door, feeling older than the moon outside the window. I closed my eyes, and images sped by like passing roadside trees. Moses carrying a stack of button-less white shirts. Moses sitting next to me at lunchtime. The flash of his smile. His hands on the rough-grained table. The hands reminded me of my father's, how they reached down a bolt of cloth from the shelf in his shop. Once I let that image in, black rags blew across desert sands. Flesh-covered bones rotted in the sun. A Turkish soldier held a bloody bayonet.

Moses glanced up at me and spoke quietly. "The wire factory failed. My mother died. Boghosian hired me part-time, and trained me. When business picked up, I started working full-time. His daughter was ready to marry, and I needed a wife."

His head was still bowed. I wanted to hear his story, and I didn't want to hear it. He didn't owe me any explanation. I hardly remembered him.

"I gave her the ring," he said.

The silver thimble was in my sewing basket.

Looking up at me, and as though reading my mind, he said, "I gave you the thimble, because you already wore a ring." Then he held out his hand and said, "Do you recognize these?"

In his palm were two large mother-of-pearl buttons from Ohanessian's.

"I took them from your tray the last day you were there," he said. "Here, one of these is for you."

He took my hand and closed the button in my fist. Then his arms were around me, I felt his shoulders under my palms, and our mouths found each other.

I thought the world would crack open and swallow us. That we would fall into a fiery furnace and burn, and not even Jesus could have saved us. I never told anyone, not even Arsinee.

Still holding me, Moses whispered into my ear, "God will forgive us for one moment of happiness."

He paused, then asked, "You named the boy for me, didn't you?"

I didn't answer.

"Moses?" It was Anahit calling from their bedroom.

Moses stepped back quickly. He looked into my eyes and then away. "Yes?"

"Are you coming to bed?" Anahit's tone was plaintive and threatening at once.

"I'm coming." Moses turned to his fate.

In the silence, I heard my own breath thunder like waves on the shore. After their door clicked shut, I returned to our room. I stood over the crib, looking at Joy, who slept peacefully, then covered Jack with a blanket. Their small bodies were so full of hope and possibility, and I wished I could protect them from disappointment.

After dropping the button into my pocket, I pulled off my dress and slip and dragged the nightgown over my head. I plucked the pins from my hair and let the braid uncoil. Trying not to disturb Jack, I slid into bed and felt gravity pressing me to the face of the planet. The earth was spinning slowly under me. I didn't want to think about Moses sleeping in the next room with his queen of beauty. I didn't want to think of Toros a floor below in blue striped pajamas that I had ironed the wrinkles from.

Ghosts from the desert were clamoring at the edge of my dreams. To get any rest at all, I'd have to drive out those memories. There was an old woman in our church in Watertown who was known for riding a white stallion in the old country. She wielded a long, leather whip and a big sword she had inherited when her husband was killed. It was said that during the massacres, she saved her family by chasing down Turks on that horse. When the fear overtook me, I closed my eyes and imagined I was old *Digin* Boyajian as a fierce warrior on a white stallion. She had the same family name I was born to.

Maybe Moses was right, and God had already forgiven us. God's face appeared before me, but it was not a kind face. I blotted it out. I pushed everything out of my head—the way I flung a basin of dirty water over the porch railing—and fell asleep.

"Ma," Moses whispered. "I can't sleep. Move over."

Without waking entirely, I shifted closer to Jack, and Moses climbed into the bed beside me.

"Tell me a story." He nestled into me like a spoon.

I remembered where I was and what had happened. "There was, there was not, there was a girl named Zabelle . . ."

"That's you," he said.

"She lived in the old country, where sheep danced down the streets and birds nested in the old ladies' hair."

"You're making that up," he commented sleepily.

I hugged him closer. "Yes, I'm making it up. True stories are too sad for little boys."

There was no response, and his breathing was slow and measured. For a long while I lay holding my sleeping son.

The next morning, I woke up between my two boys. How would it feel to see Moses and his wife? Would Toros take one look at my face and know that I had betrayed him? I heard Arsinee's voice in my head: "Toros wouldn't notice if you shaved your head bald, how is he going to see that glint of guilt in your eye?" She was right. My husband didn't pay much attention to the weather on a person's face. It was Moses Chahasbanian who knew when clouds traversed my brow. And Moses Bodjakanian who could read my heart.

My tolerance for Vartanoush's snide comments had evaporated. If she criticized me for letting Moses sleep in my bed, I would bark back at her. Fortunately, as soon as she woke up, the old woman shuffled downstairs to help prepare breakfast.

I dressed the children in their best clothes. It was Easter, the church would be full, and Christ was seated at the right hand of God. Even if God was a harsh judge, I knew Jesus would intercede on my behalf. He had been a man himself and knew about temptation and frailty. I imagined myself as Mary Magdalene, throwing myself at his feet.

As I led the children down the flight of stairs, a small voice whispered in my ear.

You could have died in the desert, but you didn't. You could have been taken as a slave, or been married to a vicious man. Your table is laden with food. Your children are healthy, and they have many choices ahead of them. What purpose is there in imagining another life any more than closing your hand over a piece of broken glass?

That wasn't Arsinee's voice. I wasn't sure who it was giving me such advice. Maybe Jesus. Maybe the spirit of my mother.

We sat at the dining-room table with the Boghosian family. I put the baby into the high seat, while Jack's chair was rigged up with a wooden crate and a belt. We ate eggs and toast and jam on white plates with hand-painted violets. Conversation moved around me like currents of air. Not a word out of Moses. I didn't look at him. I didn't look at *Digin* Big Nose.

"Last night was the first time Joy slept through. There must be something magic about the crib." I was surprised by how calm and natural my voice sounded.

"My husband hasn't managed to give us any purpose for that crib. I'm glad someone can use it," Anahit said bitterly.

There was silence around the table. No one chewed the food in his mouth. Moses stared at his lap. His ears were red. I felt his humiliation as if it were my own. Why didn't Moses slap that small, cruel mouth? How could Boghos Boghosian allow his daughter to speak that way? We continued to eat in wretched silence. Jack began to squirm in his seat, then slid so the belt came up under his armpits and his feet dangled. I rescued the child and dropped him in Vartanoush's lap.

After excusing myself from the table, I proceeded to the kitchen, with my Moses close behind.

"Ma, what did she mean? How come everybody got so mad?"

Sometimes I wished that Moses had taken after his father, instead of being so attuned to the ebb and flow of adult emotion. I sighed. I spied a basket of colored eggs on the kitchen counter. "Do you want me to teach you the secret of picking a winning egg?"

My son was not usually so easy to divert, but he had been badgering me about how I always won the Easter egg-cracking contest. "Tell me!"

Just then Moses Bodjakanian walked into the kitchen. There were dark circles around his eyes, and his shoulders sagged under an invisible weight. There was almost nothing in him of the boy from Ohanessian's, with his quick step and easy laughter.

My sympathy surged into anger. What kind of man would allow his wife to talk to him like that? How could the boy with beautiful hands have turned into this henpecked bald fellow? I picked up an egg. It was all I could do to keep myself from throwing it at Moses Bodjakanian.

"You have to find where the air bubble is," I told my son. "It depends how the egg was lying in the pot. The best is to find an egg with a small air bubble on one side, not on either end."

"How can you tell where it is?"

"Like this," I said. I tapped the end of an egg against my front tooth. "You can hear and feel the hollow spot." I handed the boy the egg.

"Who taught you?" asked little Moses.

"My father," I replied, "when I was much smaller than you are now." As the words left my mouth, the image of an egg in my father's palm floated back to me.

Little Moses tapped the shell against his tooth. Next he tapped the other end. "The space is in the bottom!"

"Right," I said, reaching for another egg. Moses Bodjakanian stretched his hand toward the basket at the same moment, and our hands brushed. A current rushed up my arm. My anger faded to pity, and then longing. What a wasteful thing the human heart is. I avoided his eyes.

Moses Bodjakanian, cradling a red egg in his hand, said, "If only one could choose everything with such care and precision, there would be less trouble in the world."

Little Moses intently tapped another egg against his tooth. He wasn't paying attention to our conversation.

I glanced at Moses Bodjakanian and then away. "Sometimes God, or fate, or circumstance, makes our choices for us."

"Then we must live with those choices," Moses said.

I looked into his solemn face. Shrugging, we both raised our shoulders, tipped our heads, and turned up our wrists. The sameness of our gestures almost made me smile.

"I found a good one!" shouted little Moses.

The boy handed the egg to me. I checked it and agreed. I said, "Now I'm going to show you another trick." I gripped the egg tightly, its tip just showing in the circle made by my thumb and forefinger. "Squeeze as tight as you can, and always try to get the other person to hit your egg, and not the other way around."

"I'm going to win!" Moses said happily. Suddenly his face clouded. "You haven't told anyone else?"

"No," I said, closing his fingers around the prize egg. "It's our secret."

After that Easter, Moses Bodjakanian and I never saw each other again.

CHAPTER EIGHT

The Conversion

(WATERTOWN, 1941)

By the time Joy graduated from the crib to a bed, I had taken command of the kitchen. Vartanoush's eyesight was failing, and she had little sense of taste. She still seemed as strong and stubborn as a donkey, though. I expected she would outlive me, if only for spite.

Even if she did give up the ghost before me, I was sure Vartanoush's decline would be a long and noisy one that we all suffered. Instead, one morning, when she didn't appear at the breakfast table, I climbed to the attic and found her cold as stone in her bed. She hadn't been laid up with illness a day since I had known her, but she was old. Years of bitterness had weakened her heart.

No one was shocked by her death, except Toros. He wandered through the rooms of the house, silent and dry-eyed. We didn't dare talk to him. Then, a week after his mother's burial, my husband came down with a mysterious malady. He burned with fever. His arms and legs were brittle as stale breadsticks, and his joints swelled like overripe figs.

Dr. Avakian huffed into the apartment, carrying a black leather bag filled with instruments and ointments. He told me he didn't know what was the matter with Toros and prescribed some pills. *Der Hayr* from the Saint James Church—the same *Der Hayr* who said words over Vartanoush's casket—came to intone some prayers. He anointed Toros with holy oil, but my husband's condition remained the same.

Later in the week the fever went down, but Toros didn't feel any better. He stayed in bed, the blinds drawn and his face turned toward the wall. We were observing the forty-day mourning for Vartanoush, so visitors filed in and out of the house. Platters and casserole dishes covered the dining-room table and the pantry counters. The sounds of eating and conversation must have filtered under his door, but Toros didn't come out of the darkened room.

Three old ladies from the church sat like crows on a telephone wire, bunched together at one end of the couch. Whispering loudly enough for everyone to hear, they said that the undertaker hadn't properly closed Vartanoush's eyes. They said that her ghost was pulling Toros toward the grave. This made me so mad, I was ready to dig that woman up and give her what she had coming to her. I also wanted to chase those old aunties off with a broom.

Toros wouldn't allow anyone in his room but me. He pushed the food I brought him from one side of the plate to the other. Keep the kids away from the door, he growled, their noise disturbs my rest. When I mentioned the market, he groaned and turned his back to me.

Moses, who wouldn't speak to us in Armenian since he'd started junior high school, wrote a big sign in English saying the store was closed until further notice. I gave Moses the keys, and he took Jack and Joy with him down the block to hang the sign in the front window. I told them they could each choose a candy bar from the counter. I would follow later to throw away what would rot on the shelves.

I had never written a check in my life. I didn't know how much money we had or where he kept it. I prayed that he would recover before the bills came due. But he just faded deeper into the pillows. His eyes were like dried-out prunes, and each breath whistled through his nose and rattled in his throat. He asked me to sleep on the couch, because he could rest better that way. Then he requested a bedpan, because he didn't want to get up and go to the bathroom. That was the last straw.

I shut myself in the bathroom to brush my hair and think. What should I do? How could I get my husband to join us back in the land of the living? I wound up the long strands from the brush and set a match to a small nest of hair.

The next day, when Toros tossed the newspaper to the floor without opening it, I phoned Arsinee. She called in sick to her job at the Edison Electric Illuminating Company and rushed over. Arsinee and I dragged four carpets and the rug beater into the yard, out of Toros's earshot.

"What did Avakian say?" Arsinee batted at a rug draped over the clothesline's wooden frame.

"He doesn't know what's the matter. The fever's gone, but Toros is worse. What am I going to do?" I groaned. "First Mother, and now this."

"You should be happy to be rid of that old screech owl, may she rest in peace," Arsinee said. She pulled the rug down.

"Don't speak of the dead like that," I said. I glanced around the yard and at the porch uneasily. The long shadow of Vartanoush's ghost hung over us.

"She was worse than a stone in your shoe. Thank the Lord she didn't put nails in your coffin. My husband was in the ground before forty, and my mother-in-law is as healthy as a heifer and twice as loud. My father-in-law will never die. He's like an old country villager who lives to one hundred and twenty."

When Arsinee's husband had died suddenly of a heart attack, she sold his store and took a job at Edison as a telephone operator to support her family. Toros was shuffling down the cemetery road, I had no idea about money, and I would be a miserable telephone operator.

"Oh, my God," Arsinee said impatiently, "would you stop crying."

I started crying harder.

Arsinee dropped the rug beater and grabbed me by the shoulders. "Come on! Act like a man, or at least remember you're a mother."

"Who's going to run the store? How will I pay the bills?" I saw myself and my children cast out onto the street, forced to beg for bread.

"He's probably got money in a cracker tin, and the rest of it stashed in the bulgur jar. Anyway, he's not dead yet."

"What can I do?" I asked.

"What is he, fifty years old?" Arsinee demanded.

"Forty-nine." I blew my nose.

"He's got twenty or thirty years left, Lord help you. Don't let his rank-smelling weed of a mother drag him into the next world."

"She's dead, and still that witch—"

Arsinee interrupted. "Don't whine. Like I said, he's not dead yet."

When I brought Toros his lunch, he waved it away. I asked him how he was feeling. He said, "Pharisees, Turks, money-lenders, politicians, barkeepers . . ." He trailed off. A fat black fly landed on his nose, and he didn't even bother to brush it away. I swatted at it. "Leave me be," he said.

While Toros lay on his deathbed, I searched for money.
I looked in the canisters, the bread box. I took off my shoes
and stood on the pantry counter, feeling around the top shelves.
I found a cache of quarters, dimes, and nickels in an old creamer
on the top shelf, but I had put that there myself. I realized I
was looking in the wrong places. I went through Toros's desk
and found all sorts of papers—fire insurance for the store, the
deed to the store, the deed to the house, the cemetery deed, a
bank passbook. I didn't have the nerve to open up the passbook and see how much was in there.

I decided that the children would help me drag Toros
from his coffin of a bed. That evening, instead of taking his
dinner in myself, I sent Joy and Jack, whom Toros hadn't seen
in days. Both of them were a little afraid of their father.

"I want you to sit on the bed and talk to him," I told them.
If his own big-eyed babies—on the brink of poverty and starvation—weren't reason enough for Toros to get out of bed and
go back to the store, I didn't know what was.

"What should we say?" asked Joy, nervously twisting a
long strand of hair around her finger.

"It doesn't matter. Ask him how he's feeling." I suddenly
imagined Toros launching into a list of complaints. "No, don't
do that. Tell him what you did in school today."

The children lingered outside the bedroom door. Joy bal-
anced a tray of food, and Jack carried a glass of *tahn*, a mixture
of yogurt and water.

Joy said, "He's going to yell."

Jack added with a note of hope, "Maybe he's too sick."

From the kitchen I urged, "Go on!" I came and stood behind them.

When they entered the darkened room, Toros switched on the bedside lamp. His face was all hollows and bones in the light and shadows. The kids sidled closer to each other.

"Put the tray here," Toros said weakly, gesturing to a table by the bed. "Come sit next to me."

Joy set down the tray, and Jack, one step behind her, leaned to put down the glass. He tripped over Joy's foot, and the *tahn* shot across the blanket and across the front of Toros's nightshirt. The glass dropped from Jack's hand and smashed on the floor. The boy covered his ears.

Toros, with more energy than he had shown in weeks, roared, "Zabelle! Get them out of here. Bring me a clean shirt! Clean up this mess!" He collapsed back onto the pillows. "Even on his deathbed, a man can't get any peace!"

On Saturday morning Dr. Avakian showed up again with his bag. I wiped the already spotless kitchen counters while I waited for his report. Finally Avakian appeared. He nodded gravely and tugged on his striped suspenders, which seemed to be holding his belly in place.

"Do you want some coffee, Doctor?" I asked.

"Thank you, *Digin* Chahasbanian."

"Sit down, sit down." I rushed into the pantry and uncovered a plate of *ghurabia,* which I set on the table.

"How is he, Doctor?" I asked, pouring him a cup of coffee.

"Not any better, not any worse," the doctor said as he bit into a cookie. "The rash, the stiffness in his bones, and the weakness of his heart are all the same. It's strange with cases like this, because tomorrow he might be up and around, or he could be. . . ." He ate another cookie. "It's like he has one foot in this world and one in the next."

I stared at the doctor's mouth. White powdered sugar clung to his lips, and a small piece of walnut dangled from his mustache. He picked up a third *ghurabia.*

"If you don't mind my saying. . . . ," he continued.

"Tell me, Doctor. . . ."

"These are excellent cookies, and I'd love to get your recipe for my wife."

"Of course. I'll write it down for you. But what about Toros?"

He replied, "I suspect this illness might have something to do with his mother." The piece of walnut dropped to his lower lip and disappeared with a flick of his tongue.

"What can we do?" I asked. I saw him eyeing the cookies and wanted to slap his pudgy hand as it reached for more.

"Well, *Digin,*" the doctor said, pocketing three cookies as he rose to go, "pray, and try to cheer him up. Give him some of these delicious cookies. That might spark his interest in life."

* * *

Arsinee arrived with Henry and Dahlia in the afternoon. From the front porch we watched the kids raking fallen leaves on the lawn. Dahlia pretended she was shot and toppled into a pile of leaves. Moses and Henry buried her and Jack, while Joy stood to the side, cheering them on. They were having fun for the first time since Vartanoush's funeral. But when they got noisy, I thought it would bother Toros, and I made them go in the garage.

I told Arsinee what the doctor said.

"Some genius Avakian is," Arsinee remarked. "Did he have any ideas about how to get that skunk cabbage's arms from around your husband's neck?"

"I wish there were a pill for it," I said.

"In the old country, a healer would come and send Vartanoush's ghost over the bridge of hair into the afterlife. Maybe we should do it. Sprinkle some salt, a little holy water, say a few words . . ."

"Toros would kill me if he found out."

"Are you going to let her drag him into the next world without a fight? We'll do it while he's sleeping."

I was ready to try anything. "Do what?" I asked.

"Leave it to me. I'll talk to *Digin* Haygouhi. She lives by me. Her mother was a healer in the mountains near Zeytoun."

"Is she still alive? She must be over a hundred."

"She sweeps the sidewalk every day, and lives on *tahn.* See if you can get Toros to drink some."

"He needs something stronger than yogurt to wake him up," I commented gloomily. "Like kerosene."

Arsinee laughed and patted me on the back. "That's the spirit."

It was late evening toward the middle of the next week, and Toros wasn't any better. I checked out the front window for Arsinee, who had called as she was leaving to say she was on her way. Joy and Jack were in bed, and Moses was at the dining-room table, finishing his homework. I watched his pencil move across the paper. His hair shone gold under the lamp. I knew he was worried about his father and about the store. But at that moment I needed him out of the way.

"Moses, you should go to bed," I said.

"Ma, I'm thirteen years old. It's early," he protested.

"Be a good boy. You can read in bed. Make sure you shut the light. Edison is richer than me."

Moses gathered up his books and papers. He stopped at the stairs leading to the attic. "Ma, you think Pa's going to get better?"

I went to him, resting my hand on his head. His eyes were always serious, even when he was a baby. Would he have to quit school and take a job delivering coal to keep us from the poorhouse?

"Pa's going to be all right, honey. Go to bed."

Just as Moses disappeared up the stairs, Arsinee arrived.

She carried a pillowcase that bulged in all directions. "I've got everything we need," she said, dropping onto the sofa.

I imagined a sheep's head, curling chicken feet, a vial of cypress oil, some dried leaves. Maybe a shriveled umbilical cord and some fingernail parings.

"First thing, we bundle up all Vartanoush's belongings, and burn them," said Arsinee.

"We can't do that!" I saw a bonfire shooting flames into the night sky. How would I explain a charred patch in the back-yard to Toros?

"All right. It won't be as good, but we can shove them in a closet in the attic. Next we scatter salt in the corners of her room, and in Toros's room. We sprinkle some holy water on Toros."

I was so nervous, my palms were perspiring. I wiped them on my skirt.

She continued, "Then you make sure he wears something blue every day for a week. There's more, but I'll explain as we go along."

"Did *Digin* Haygouhi tell you this?"

"She's a little mixed up—her mind's not so good any-more—but I got the idea. I remembered a few things myself."

"This has the devil's hand in it."

"Oh, hush up. You want to save your husband or not?"

"I think he's asleep."

Arsinee snorted. "I can hear the snoring from here."

We snuck to Vartanoush's room in the attic. Arsinee tied up the dresses inside a sheet. I emptied the bureau drawers and stuffed the pillowcases. I stopped to look at the things in the top drawer—a cracked hand mirror, a gilt-edged comb, a stack of bookmarks inscribed with Bible verses, a stray hairpin. I fingered a black button that had fallen off the old lady's favorite sweater the day before she died. It was true she had been a thorn in my side. Still, there were times when she had been sweet to the children. Over the years, Vartanoush had become part of my life the way a sticky cabinet door did. You grew accustomed to jerking the handle in a particular way, and if the door somehow began opening easily, it would take awhile to unlearn the old trick. I slipped the button into my pocket and returned to work.

In the back of the drawer, behind a worn copy of the Armenian Bible, there was a knotted gray sock. I undid the sock and shook out its contents. A brooch—a wreath of blue stones dotted with small pearls—glittered in my palm. This was the only piece of jewelry Toros had ever given me.

It was my tenth wedding anniversary gift. The pin had disappeared a few weeks later. Toros had accused me of misplacing it or losing it, but I knew I had left it on the lapel of my coat. I searched every corner of the house, every pocket, every drawer, except for Vartanoush's room. My mother-in-law had suggested that the clasp might have loosened and the pin might have fallen into the street. Maybe this was God's way of letting me know I shouldn't take pride in material things, she had said. The old harpy had hidden the pin in her drawer for all those years.

I squeezed the brooch until the settings dug into my hand. I felt steam rushing through my veins. I fished the button from my pocket, dropped it onto the floor, and stomped on it with the heel of my shoe.

Arsinee grabbed my arm. "*Khent es?* You're making enough noise to wake the dead. Come on, help me."

We bound up a second sheet filled with Vartanoush's things and heaved it into a musty walk-in closet in the hall.

Joy opened her bedroom door, rubbing her eyes. "What you doing, Ma?"

"Putting away some of Grandma's things, honey." I shooed her back to bed.

Next we opened the windows and spread salt in the four corners of the old lady's room. Then we tiptoed down the stairs and into Toros's room. His snores rumbled from among the bedclothes.

I held a candle while Arsinee rummaged in the pillow-case. She pulled a horseshoe from the sack.

"This," she whispered, "we put under the mattress."

"*Digin* Haygouhi told you that?"

"I heard it somewhere. Don't worry, it'll help." She slid the horseshoe smoothly into place. Toros snored on. "Salt next," Arsinee instructed.

It bothered me a little, knowing I'd have to sweep it up the next day. But I tossed salt into the corners and opened the closet door and threw some in there for good measure.

"Now, while you douse him with holy water, I'll say a few words." Arsinee unscrewed the lid on a Mason jar and handed it to me.

"This is holy water?" I whispered.

"It's holy enough."

I raised an eyebrow. "Where did you get it?"

Arsinee said, "Out of the birdbath."

I put the candle on the bureau and tiptoed toward the bed, the jar in hand.

Arsinee whispered, "Hear, O Vartanoush, we command you, in the name of the Lord, to leave this room. . . ."

I whispered, "The *Digin* told you to say that?"

Arsinee went on. "To leave this house. Cross the bridge of hair from this world into the next. Go to your Maker, and leave Toros here with his wife and children. . . ."

I let a few drops fall onto Toros's bed. He continued to snore, and I grew bolder dropping some water onto his forehead.

He paused midsnore. He said, "What? Who?"

I backed away from the bed.

"It's your mother, Toros," whispered Arsinee.

Arsinee sounded just like Vartanoush. I couldn't believe my ears.

"*Mayrig?*" he asked sleepily.

What if Toros woke up and found us strewing his room with salt and magic spells, talking in the voice of his dead mother?

"Yes, *yavrum,*" continued Arsinee. "I'm leaving, Toros, but you must stay here. You must provide for your wife and children. Don't abandon them, son."

"No, *Mayrig,*" he said, drifting back into sleep.

Arsinee pointed toward the hall, and the two of us went out, closing the door softly behind.

When we reached the living room, I said, "You almost gave me a heart attack. You sounded just like her. It was our good luck that he didn't wake up."

"Well, that takes care of her," said Arsinee. "*Bitdi, getdi,*" she added, gesturing as though to brush flour from her hands.

"I hope so," I said. I patted the brooch in my pocket.

The next morning I was ready for him to yell at me about the salt, the water, the horseshoe, the whole crazy thing. When I opened the door to his room, a cold blast of air hit me. He had pulled up the shade, and the window was wide open. He was standing in the middle of the room, and I rushed past him to shut the sash. He would catch pneumonia like that.

Then I turned to him. He stood, a wild halo of hair around his head, his eyes snapping like matches, smiling.

"I have seen the Lord, Zabelle. He was in the pear tree," he said to me.

I put my hand to my heart and closed my eyes. His body was healed, but now he had lost his mind. Jesus in the pear tree. Toros had snapped. It was Arsinee's fault. I opened my eyes and saw an idiot's joy spread across my husband's face. I thought we would have to send him to the mental hospital. I wanted to faint.

"Don't look at me like that!" He laughed. "I saw Jesus, and he told me to join the *poghokagans* to build His true church."

I was speechless. The *poghokagans?* What did the Protestants have to do with anything? This was the result of *Digin* Haygouhi's spells. God was punishing us.

He explained it all to me. How he jumped out of bed in the morning, opened the shade, and saw Jesus in the pear tree. Jesus was dressed in long robes, and He said, in these exact words, "Toros, I have healed you that you might build Me a new church."

So my husband, who was one of the founders of the Saint James Armenian Apostolic Church, vowed to join the Armenian Brethren and help them build their new church. It was a divine revelation, like something out of the Old Testament or Saul's conversion on the road to Damascus. Saul was from Tarsus, which was very close to Adana, Toros's hometown.

Given my husband's leanings toward Bible-thumping sermons and direct communication with God, our belonging to the

Armenian Brethren Church on Arlington Avenue made sense. No liturgy, no long black robes and enormous crosses, just the Bible, "Bringing in the Sheaves" in Armenian, and straight, hard pews. It was the same Bible and, as far as I could tell, the same God, in either place. The only sad part for me was that Arsinee and I weren't in the same house of worship on Sunday. But we had all week to gab about twice as many people.

After he told me about his vision, Toros grabbed me by the hands and twirled me around. "I'm on fire with the Spirit of the Lord," he said.

In the moment, I decided not to question him. Maybe Jesus had spoken to him. Maybe the salt had worked, and Vartanoush's spirit had been banished from our house. At least he was out of bed. I tried to figure out some way to get him to wear blue for the rest of the week.

By this time the kids stood in the doorway, watching us, not sure what to think.

"Come on, Moses!" shouted Toros. "Let's go down to the store." He hustled Moses and the other two children out of the house, saying they'd be back by lunch. The kids were happy— I heard them laughing down the stairs and out onto Lincoln Street.

I flung open the window and stood in the cold air, brushing my hair. A squirrel stared at me from the top branches of the pear tree. I hurled the hairbrush at the bushy-tailed rat, which leaped down the tree and scurried out of sight. Then I went to fetch the broom.

CHAPTER NINE

The Work of the Lord

(CHICAGO, 1948)

I marked the passage of time with a pencil on a door frame. My children shot up faster than seedlings in a summer garden. Moses was twenty, Jack was a teenager, and my baby was beginning to have a woman's body. It seemed like one minute I was in the basement, hanging out row upon row of diapers, and the next minute I was presiding at a dinner table of creatures half human, half beast—Americans.

Moses was turned down by the army because of flat feet, and I was very thankful for those feet. He wanted to go to Bible school and train to be a preacher. Moses had never been interested in the market, and Toros had long since settled on Jack to take over the store when the time came. Since he'd been ten Jack had helped out at the market, while Moses had gone to the town library to study.

Sometimes Moses wrote sermons for his imaginary church, and when he asked, I would be his congregation. He was a marvel to listen to, my Moses, his words as sturdy and beautiful as an old country church. The preacher in him came in part from his father's dinner-table ranting, but he was gentle as well. He could have persuaded a wolf in a sheep fold to eat grass rather than lamb.

After he finished high school, Moses took a job selling encyclopedias. The company van scooped up the salesmen and dropped them in nearby suburbs, where they went house to house. Once Moses overcame his fear of rapping on doors and greeting unknown ladies of the house, he outsold the other boys on his team. Saving every penny, he guarded his bankbook like it was the key to the Holy Kingdom. Toros was extremely proud and pushed Moses to apply to the Moody Bible Institute in Illinois.

When the letter from Chicago pitched through the mail slot, I was home alone. The envelope was thick with promise or disaster, depending on your point of view. I had a notion to get my garden spade and bury the thing under the spruce in the front yard. But I couldn't do that to my son. When Moses sat down to dinner that night, the envelope lay on his plate. He was so happy, he kept slapping his face and laughing. Jack whooped like a wild man, and I thought Toros was going to start jumping around like a kid. Joy looked at me nervously. She knew it was going to break my heart.

Then the morning came for him to take his new leather suitcase and leave us. I tried to be cheerful, but every time I thought about my Moses, my first baby, going halfway across the country to live with strangers, I had to pull the handkerchief out of my purse and wipe my eyes.

"Ma," said Jack from the backseat, "would you turn the faucet off?"

"Why don't you leave her alone," Joy said.

"Think of Hannah in the Bible," Toros said. "She gave Samuel up to the Lord when he was a small child. Our Moses is a grown man."

I put the handkerchief over my face.

Toros talked to Moses. "When you finish, maybe you could be pastor of our church. Who knows, though, what God has planned. You could be called to the mission fields. Africa, India, South America . . ."

I started crying harder. I felt as though someone were sawing at my right leg, cutting it off below the joint. How did I raise him to be the leaving kind? Jack and Joy would stay close by, the old country way, but I could feel Moses lifting anchor.

Jack said, "Ma, calm down. They have telephones in Chicago."

"He'll be back in the summer, Ma," Joy added.

". . . to preach to the heathen in the jungle. You would do great work in the mission field," Toros continued, "although we could use a revival here in America. There is work to be done among the heathen in this country."

When we reached the station, Jack lugged Moses's suitcases to the platform, where we stood in a small dark knot by the waiting train. Moses looked uncomfortable, as though he wanted to sneak away and pretend he didn't know us. I had no intention of causing a fuss. Toros continued yammering in Armenian at Moses, who no longer spoke a word of his mother tongue.

Although Moses had stopped speaking Armenian when he was twelve, he never pretended he didn't understand us when we spoke it, which some kids did. He answered us in English, and soon Jack picked up the trick. That was how the Armenians would be finished off. First we were driven out, then the children abandoned the language, and finally they married *odars* and birthed children who were barely half Armenian. But I'm getting ahead of myself here.

As I stood on the train platform, Moses's childhood unrolled in my head like a tapestry. I remembered rocking him in the night when he was sick, and the dusky baby smell that clung to his soft hair. How he clasped my hand tightly as we crossed the street on the way to his first day at school, his unscuffed brown shoes a source of pride to us both. Now he stood there, almost a grown man, as bright as a new copper penny, all that was the best about us about to be flung into the world's coffer.

It reminded me of a summer day years before when I took the kids to Revere Beach on the streetcar. Jack brought a kite with him, which leaped into the full wind like a bird. He let out more and more string, until the kite was only a colored speck near the sun. I told him to reel it back in, that otherwise he might lose it, but he didn't care. He felt the tug in his hands as it made for the heavens. He wanted to see how high it could go. And then the string snapped. He was probably eight or nine at the time, and tough as he was, his face crumpled into despair. But still, I don't think he would have done any differently.

"He learned his first Bible verse before he could read," Toros stated. Who was he talking to? It was like this was some kind of testimonial dinner or he was delivering Moses' eulogy.

Joy produced a flat package she had concealed under her coat. She held it out to Moses, saying shyly, "I made this for you."

Moses undid the paper to find a pair of hand-knit socks in fine navy wool. He pulled on one of Joy's braids. "Thanks, sis," he said huskily.

When the whistle blew, Moses hugged Joy and shook hands with Toros and Jack, while I stood to one side. Then he leaned down to hug me. He was stiff and unyielding, but I couldn't help holding on to him like he was a wooden plank in the bobbing sea. I imagined myself gripping the hem of his coat as he mounted the train steps, dragging behind him. He pulled himself free and slowly picked up his suitcase.

Suddenly I was a small, dirt-caked girl among a hundred ragged children, reaching up to Moses, begging for a crust of bread. But with dignity and determination, he climbed the steps of the train, knowing he could save only himself. Like a fox in an iron trap, he would chew off his own leg in order to make his escape.

I called after him, "Moses, don't forget us."

The train pulled out of the station, and he was gone.

* * *

The next day Arsinee came over to keep me company. I had run through a half dozen or more handkerchiefs, with no end in sight. All sensible thoughts had flown out of my head, and I was crazy as a hen whose chick had been snatched by a weasel.

"I should have killed him the day he was born," I sobbed.

"That's a nice way for a mother to talk," said Arsinee.

"I knitted his bones inside my body. I chewed up food and put it in his mouth. And now he's gone. He's left the only home he's ever known." I wanted sympathy, not smart comments.

"They learn that in this country. You still have the other two, which is a lot more than some people. Besides, Chicago isn't that far."

"What do you know? Henry moved three miles to Boston, and Dahlia will never go farther than the next block."

"I hardly see them."

I sniffed into my handkerchief. "If we lived in the old country, he would have married a nice girl, and we'd all be living in the same house. In this country, all they can think of is trains and planes taking you as far as you can get from your mother."

"Maybe if you hadn't nursed him until he was five years old, he would have stayed closer to home," Arsinee said.

"Some friend you are. My heart is being devoured by jackals, and you crack jokes."

Arsinee, "Honey, the world is claiming him, and you have to move over."

"Move over into my grave," I retorted.

"You don't have enough white hairs to count, and you're talking about the grave. Maybe that's the best place for you if you're going to be sitting in ashes, tearing out your hair. Come on. Stop feeling sorry for yourself."

I dreamed about Moses that night. I stood on the sidewalk in a strange city, watching a parade go by. He was marching down the street in a beige uniform with red trim, waving a baton, with hundreds of boys following him. They all looked alike— same height, build, blond hair, same blank stare—and they were singing "Onward Christian Soldiers." I could tell my son from them because he had the only distinctive profile. I waved and called, "Moses! Moses!" But he didn't stop for a minute. He didn't even glance my way. He just kept marching at the head of the troop. I wanted to run after him, but my shoes were stuck to the pavement with a thick glue, and I couldn't lift my feet. Those boys marched right down the street to the ocean, onto a pier, and off the pier into the harbor.

I woke up in a worse mood than I had been in the day before. We hadn't heard a word from Moses, and he was definitely in Chicago by that time. I woodenly made preparations for the midday meal before leaving for church. The sermon was something about brotherly love, and it flew in one ear and out the other like my head was a rotted-out tree stump. Unfortunately the closing hymn for the day was "Amazing Grace"—in Armenian—and I broke down because it was Moses's favorite. I had to run from the pew to the ladies' room, where I perched on the toilet seat cover and wept.

When we sat down to dinner, I noticed that Joy had automatically set a place for Moses. His empty chair, the unused plate and fork and knife, it took my appetite away.

Toros shouted, "The boy hasn't died, Zabelle. He's gone to do the Lord's work."

"I almost wish he were dead, because then I wouldn't have to worry about him. He'd be in heaven, instead of in some town hundreds of miles away among foreigners, eating strange food. He could be lying by the roadside right now, clubbed over the head by a robber, bleeding in the gutter, and we wouldn't know it."

Jack and Joy stared at Toros. I didn't need to look to know that the muscle in his jaw had begun to twitch, which wasn't a good sign.

But I couldn't stop myself. It was as if I had a part in a play, and I just had to say my lines, no matter what. I continued, "He could be dead for all we know."

Toros slammed his fist on the table, rattling the glasses and silver. He thundered, "I won't stand for any more of this gnashing of teeth. He's a grown man."

My mouth snapped shut. What did Toros know? Only a mother could understand what it was to lose a child.

* * *

A week went by, and still no word from Moses. There were hours when I was able to stuff a tray of tomatoes and green peppers without once thinking of him. I'd have my feet propped up on the hassock in the living room, reading the Bible, when the mail thumped to the floor in the front hall. I'd spread the envelopes like a fan and find nothing. The dread of his absence would cleave me in half, like a melon on a cutting board. I slumped into a chair, without the energy to push back a lock of hair fallen across my forehead. After a time, I forced myself to go to the basement and fold the laundry. When Joy came home from school, she and I walked to the store to visit Toros and Jack.

Finally one afternoon a postcard arrived saying, "Ma and Pa, Arrived safely. Will call when I get a chance."

"When he gets a chance?" I asked Arsinee. "Do you think he's in classes day and night? Do you think he has to walk two miles to find a telephone?"

"He's in a new world. He's twenty years old. He needs some time."

"Some time for what? To forget his mother?"

"Lord almighty, Zabelle, I'm going to shoot you and put you out of your misery."

That Sunday he called. Jack, Joy, and I crowded around the telephone table in the hall as Toros shouted into the receiver.

"Are you learning things?" he demanded. "Are they our kind of Christians?"

When it was my turn, I felt shy talking to my own son.

"Moses," I said.

"Yes, Ma."

"Are you wearing the sweater I made you?"

He laughed. "It's buttoned to my neck."

"Are you eating okay? Do they give you enough to eat?"

"There's plenty of food, Ma. Don't worry."

"What about your roommate? Is he a nice boy?"

"Bobby, uh, Robert, Lyle. He's a good guy. We get along. They're all healthy Americans here. I'm the only Armenian for miles around."

"I'm praying for you," I said.

Hearing his familiar voice gave me hope that he hadn't become a different person in two weeks' time. He was still my Moses.

Some weeks later, while Toros was at work and the kids were at school, I was in the kitchen chopping onions when the phone rang. Moses, I thought. He had called collect. He sounded so close, like he was at a pay phone down the block. His voice was strained, and I could just see him jiggling his leg up and down, the way he did when he was nervous.

"What's the matter, honey?" I asked.

"Nothing, Ma. I just wanted to ask your advice about something."

"Your roommate? How is your roommate?"

"Bobby's fine."

"Are you feeling okay?"

"I'm not sick. There's just this thing . . ."

"I can hear it in your voice. What is it?"

"Well, I don't know exactly. . . ."

When he paused, all sorts of things ran through my head. Topics a mother didn't really want to hear about, but what could I do? "Tell me, Moses."

"I heard a voice."

"A voice?"

"It woke me up, Ma. I heard someone calling my name. 'Moses. Moses.' I sat up in bed, and turned on the light. Bobby was sound asleep. I looked under the bed, even. So I shut out the light, and I heard it again."

Was this what happened to boys who went so far from home? They started hearing voices? Was Moses getting crazy?

"What did the voice say, honey?" I asked him.

"Ma, I swear, it was just like Samuel in the Bible. Remember Samuel when God spoke to him?"

"Maybe you were dreaming. What did you eat for supper? Did you eat that *basterma* I sent you? If you eat that on an empty stomach, it can give you nightmares."

"Ma, I didn't eat the meat. It makes me stink like a camel. And it wasn't a nightmare, it was God. He spoke to me and he said, 'Moses, I am calling you to be a fisher of men. You are going to be a powerful man in the Lord's work. As a tool in My Hand, you are going to evangelize the world.'"

"Moses, what makes you think it was God?" I asked him. "What did the voice sound like?"

"He sounded like a radio announcer. A radio announcer with no microphone, no transmitter, and no radio. He was speaking to me from heaven, but it sounded like he was in the room. Then he said, 'Moses, in order to do My work, you must be true and devout. You must not succumb to the temptations of the flesh. You must study hard.'"

"Are you sure it wasn't your father talking?" I asked dryly.

"Ma. I'm telling you, it was God. Like in the Bible. But what He said next was kind of weird."

I held my breath.

Moses went on, "He said, 'Moses, you must change your name from Chahasbanian to Charles.'" He paused for a moment. "Then God told me to have my nose fixed."

"What?" I asked.

"Plastic surgery, you know. Like Paul Barsamian."

"God told you to have a nose job like Paul Barsamian?"

"Not in exactly those words, but yes, that was the idea."

"That's crazy!" I shouted into the phone. "Why would God tell you to change your nose? It's a perfectly beautiful Armenian nose. It's your father's nose, and his father's nose, and his father's nose before him. Who are you going to be, Moses? What kind of person are you going to be without your name and your nose? Do you think if you try to be an *odar*, it will work? Your eyes are Armenian. Your soul is Armenian."

"Ma!" the boy pleaded. "Please stop yelling. Maybe I shouldn't have called. I don't know who to talk to. If I tell anyone here, I'm afraid they'll think I'm crazy. I couldn't believe it, either, and I asked God, 'Lord, are you sure about this?' and he said, 'Trust Me, My son. You are chosen to do a great work.'"

I wasn't sure what was going on. Either the boy had completely lost his mind or God was speaking to him—a blond-haired, small-nosed God who spoke the perfect American of a radio announcer. Moses and the burning bush. Samuel in the temple. Jesus in a pear tree. Maybe visions ran in the family, although they didn't come from my side. The poor boy sounded lonely and confused. He wanted some comfort, some reassurance. What was there to say?

He kept talking. "I've been reading the biography of Dwight Moody, Ma, the man this school is named for. He was a great evangelist, who started as a traveling salesman. But God made him a great preacher. Maybe that's what God wants for me."

"Honey," I interrupted, "is there somebody there you can talk to? Isn't there somebody who's supposed to look after the new boys?"

"Well," he said, "there's Dr. Pruitt, my adviser."

"Why don't you go talk with him?"

"Should I tell him about the nose?"

"No, don't bring that up. That can be between you and the Lord." I knew he didn't have the money to afford a plastic surgeon anyway.

So he gave me the number of a pay phone near his dorm room, and we chose a time for me to call the next day. I sat at the telephone desk after I hung up, mulling over the conversation. I wanted to talk to Arsinee, but I could already hear her wisecrack. I decided not to say anything to anybody.

That night I dreamed about my boy again. I was standing on a corner, watching him approach at the head of a Salvation Army band. He came closer and closer. I saw that his face was different. His beautiful nose was gone, and in its place was the sorriest excuse for a nose I had ever seen—a little button of a thing that turned up at the end. It made me want to cry. But his eyes hadn't changed—those dark, deep eyes that were the same as mine. I looked into them and felt myself tumbling down a silent, drafty tunnel that went on and on. I woke up with my blood thumping wildly in my neck.

The next day, when I dialed, he picked up on the first ring. His voice was firm, but he sounded far away.

"What did he say?" I asked.

"He said that it was unusual in these times for God to speak directly to a person, so I shouldn't talk about it with the other students. But that I should keep my ears and my heart open for other revelations."

"That's all?" I couldn't tell from Moses's report if the man believed him or not.

"That's it."

I sighed. Moses, who the day before had been open-mouthed and trembling, had shut tighter than a mussel. That's the way it was with children. Every step toward independence was followed by a moment of panic when they tumbled into your lap like a toddler. Two minutes later they were angry at you for holding them too tightly. The same Moses who had sought my advice the day before decided he didn't need me. He would transform himself into a small-nosed, blank-named, big-deal American evangelist. What could you do but love your children?

"Ma, I've got to go. Bobby's waiting for me in the library."

As soon as I hung up, I dialed Arsinee's number. It was busy, so I went out for a walk around the block to calm my nerves. When I passed the Italian's yard, I half expected the plaster Madonna to offer me some consoling words, but the white face remained still.

Later in the week we received another postcard written in Moses's perfect penmanship. I still have it, tied up in a faded yellow ribbon with the few cards and letters he wrote over the years.

October 1948

Dear Ma and Pa,

I finally heard the call. God spoke to me a few nights ago, and he is going to make me a great preacher like the Reverend Moody, the man who founded this school. Pray for me.

The food here is pretty bad, but the guys are nice. Say hello to Jack and Joy. Do you think you could send me some more money? My first paycheck from the library won't come through for a month.

In Christ's love,

Your son

Toros read it out loud at dinner, his chest puffed out like a great bird. He didn't even seem to mind the request for money. I imagined Moses was starting to save for his plastic surgery. How could I argue with God?

Arsinee came over the next afternoon, and I showed the card to her.

"What do you think?" I asked.

Arsinee looked at me skeptically. "God spoke to him."

I shrugged. "He's his father's son. Jesus spoke to Toros, why shouldn't God speak to Moses?"

"I'm surprised the burning bush didn't set his bed on fire."

"You should be on the radio."

"Did you write back?"

I handed Arsinee the note I had written in response.

Dear Moses

The day you were born I said you would be a great leader. God gave you your nose. Why would He take it away? The weather here is fine. We miss you.

Love,

Ma

"What's this thing about the nose?" she asked, handing it back to me.

"God told him to have plastic surgery on his nose," I said. "Don't repeat that, or I'll never speak to you again."

Arsinee laughed and slapped her thigh. "God works in mysterious ways."

"Oh, hush up," I grumbled.

"He doesn't realize, honey, that his nose will come back to haunt him on the face of his children."

That thought made me feel a little better.

"I'm sending him some food," I said, putting the note into an envelope and sliding a five-dollar bill in after it. "He's starving to death."

"Won't it be spoiled by the time it gets there? Why don't you send some *basterma?* It keeps for years."

"He won't eat it. I'm sending him *cheoregs* and *ghurabia,* plus some dried fruit."

"Maybe God will drop some manna in his room during the night."

She could make all the jokes she wanted, but somehow I knew that God's predictions for my son would come true.

CHAPTER TEN

Chahasbanian and Son

(WATERTOWN, 1953)

When Moses came home the first summer after he started Moody, he looked at me with the eyes of a stranger, judging every gesture I made. I had the impression that even the way I drank water was somehow distasteful to him. After he returned to Chicago in the fall, he never lived with us again. When we spoke on the phone, he and I were polite, as if we were neighbors chatting with each other over a fence. On good days I felt like a chrysalis from which a butterfly had emerged, and on bad days I felt like a chewing-gum wrapper someone had thrown in the hedges.

When Moses finished Bible college, he took an assistant pastor job in Pasadena, California, which was as far away from Watertown as you could get without changing continents. His fiancée was the pastor's daughter, and her name was Sarah Aiken; this much we learned from a letter. He enclosed a studio portrait of himself with an arm around a pretty, smiling brown-haired girl. I studied the photo and grudgingly had to admit that Moses's new nose suited his face well enough.

As time wore on, missing Moses faded into a mild case of rheumatism—it pained me early in the morning or if the rain fell a few days in a row. I could live with it. Then the trouble with Jack began. He had never been a talkative boy, but after he entered high school, getting words out of him at all was an effort. His replies were brief and full of gaps, like a telegraph.

When Jack turned sixteen, Toros began pestering him to quit school. As far as my husband could see, it was a waste for Jack to spend one more day at Watertown High School than the law required. With some persuading from me, Toros agreed that Jack could earn his diploma, as long as the boy showed up at the market within thirty minutes of school's close and worked on Saturdays.

Jack enjoyed careening around town in the delivery truck, but I think he missed playing on the baseball team with his friends. His easy smile and polite manner earned him good tips from the housewives up the hill. He was the handsomest of my children and the most lighthearted, which was maybe why Toros rode him so hard. The two of them charged the air with the electricity you feel before a summer storm. I was always waiting for the downpour.

As Jack's eighteenth birthday and high school graduation approached, the tension between father and son increased. Toros constantly referred to Jack as the onion head or that lazy bum. Jack paid less attention to Toros's instructions and delivered boxes to the wrong house or forgot half of somebody's order. I heard about all of this at the end of the day from Toros, who ranted at the dinner table about his good-for-nothing son as though Jack weren't sitting right there with a fork and knife in hand.

"The boy is mentally bankrupt," Toros shouted.

Joy quietly drummed her fingers on the table.

"Stop that," ordered Toros.

She flattened her palms on the tablecloth and looked at me.

"Why don't you put your feet up and read the paper, Toros. You're giving yourself indigestion," I said.

"I gotta get out of here," Jack muttered, and he was gone.

"I'll be in my room," said Joy.

"Where does he think he's going?" called Toros from his armchair.

"I don't know," I said, "and I don't care." I stomped into the kitchen to wash the dishes.

Toros was a sheepdog keeping after a wayward sheep. He circled around and around, nipping at the boy's heels and barking, which only made Jack straggle more. One morning, when Jack was late coming to the breakfast table before school, Toros shouted up the stairs.

"I'll be right down, Pa," Jack bellowed. "Tell Ma no eggs. Just toast and coffee."

"Did you hear that?" Toros asked me.

"The neighbors heard the both of you," I said.

Jack breezed into the room and straddled his chair.

Toros glared at Jack over the top of the newspaper. "A girl telephoned you last night. She said not to bother to call back because she'd see you in school."

Jack munched on his toast with his eyes down.

"So, Mr. Romance, you aren't even going to ask me the girl's name?"

Joy and I exchanged glances.

"Of course, you must know who it is, right, Jack?"

"Right," said Jack.

I poured my husband another cup of coffee, checking an impulse to dump it over his head. "Drink your juice, Jack," I said, patting my son's back.

Toros was a dog with his teeth clamped on the mailman's pant leg. "Do you know why Miss Marie Doucette was calling?"

"Help with homework," Jack mumbled.

"She would call a know-nothing for homework? You listen to me: when it's time for a wife, we'll find you a nice

Armenian girl from a good family." He went back behind his newspaper.

Jack jumped up from the table. "Bye, Ma. See you later, sis," he said, and then thundered down the back stairs.

"I'm inviting the Kalajians to come for coffee after prayer meeting tonight," Toros said.

"Pa," complained Joy, "I can't go to church tonight. I have a paper due tomorrow."

"God comes first," was the reply.

I raised my eyebrows at Joy, who shrugged and shook her head. I mouthed the words "Leave it to me." She gathered up her things and left for school.

I knew the turns of Toros's mind like I knew my linen closet. "Jack's not interested in Maral Kalajian."

"What does he know? Healthy tree, unspoiled fruit."

I wasn't going to waste my breath. "Joy's staying home tonight. I believe God approves of her doing her homework. I invited Arsinee to dinner."

Arsinee set forks and knives beside the plates on the dining-room table. She was complaining about Dahlia's husband, Chet, who worked for the Prudential Insurance Company.

"His name sounds like something you'd spit from your mouth," she called to me in the kitchen.

"You always say that," I commented. "And Henry's wife serves dirty dishwater for coffee."

Arsinee joined me beside the stove. "All we get are *odars*. Moses, Henry, Dahlia. Do you think Jack would look at an Armenian girl?"

Joy walked into the kitchen, laden with books.

"You'd go for a nice Armenian boy, wouldn't you, honey?" asked Arsinee.

Joy blushed. "Oh, Auntie, leave me alone."

"She's too young for a boyfriend," I said.

"Too young? You were married when you were her age," Arsinee said.

"Don't remind me," I replied. "Toros is dragging the Kalajians over here tonight. He's trying to fix up Jack with Maral."

"Maral?" snorted Arsinee.

"The poor thing has a mustache," I said.

"She's shaped like a pear," Arsinee added.

"How can you two be so mean?" asked Joy.

"We're not mean," protested Arsinee. "She's a sweet girl."

"Just not Jack's type," I said.

"Jack's type," Joy repeated sarcastically.

"What can you tell us, Joy?" Arsinee laughed.

Just then Toros and Jack came in, and it was time to eat. When dinner was over, Jack excused himself from the table and raced up the stairs to his bedroom.

"We're leaving in ten minutes," Toros called after him.

Joy volunteered to clear and wash the dishes, so Arsinee and I went to the living room, where Toros was reading his

Bible. We sat on the couch, and I offered Arsinee a mint from the glass bowl. Through the window I saw something moving on the front porch. Or, more precisely, over the front porch. Arsinee saw it, too, and elbowed me. We both checked Toros, who was engrossed in his reading. Jack climbed down the second-story porch, disappearing onto the porch below.

Toros put down the magazine. "Jack," he bellowed, "time to go. Get down here."

Without thinking I blurted, "I'll get him." I hurried to the attic. Sure enough, the curtain fluttered in Joy's window. I craned my head and saw my son jog down Walnut Street.

I wasn't sure why, but I told Toros that Jack didn't feel well. "He's upstairs in bed."

"What's the matter with that *esh* now?" Toros asked.

"His stomach. He'll be okay, but he needs to rest," I said.

Arsinee caught my eye and winked. I ignored her. Joy spread her books out on the dining-room table.

When the prayer meeting was over, we stood on the church steps with Hagop Kalajian, his wife, and moon-faced Maral. By chance, Toros looked up as a blue convertible sped by, driven by Jack's friend Danny Dedayan, who had his arm around a blonde. Jack and a brunette were in the backseat. Toros grabbed my arm and pointed. "There goes your rotten son! Stomachache, hah!"

I pressed my lips together and exhaled slowly through my nose.

The Kalajians fidgeted in our living room for less than an hour. They had seen Jack, and Maral was humiliated. After the company left, and Joy had gone to bed, Toros and I sat on the back porch.

"He's American, Toros, and he's a teenager. You named him Jack, not Hampartsoum."

"American! What does that mean? A good-for-nothing who defies his father?"

"It's not like the old country. They want to choose for themselves now. So they have to meet different people to get an idea."

"Fornication? Is that what you're talking about?"

"Going to the Town Diner for a hamburger, that's what I'm talking about."

"When I was his age, I was God-fearing and respectful of my elders. Did you and I go to the Town Diner? No."

No, I thought, we hadn't even laid eyes on each other when we were married. "This is the 1950s Toros, and America."

"No wonder he acts this way, with you encouraging him."

"Toros, don't be on his neck every minute, or we could lose him."

Toros harrumphed.

"You can't break him," I said. "You can only drive him underground, or away. Let me talk with him, okay?"

"I need some sleep," Toros grumbled.

After midnight Jack tiptoed through the living room. I was sitting at the bottom of the attic stairs in my robe.

"Ma! You should be in bed!"

"I should be in bed? I saw you climb down the porch, Jack. And your father spotted you in Dedayan's car."

He sat down next to me. "Sorry."

"You stink like cigarettes. Why are you sucking on filth? Your body is God's temple."

"Sorry, Ma," he said again.

"Why not a girl from the church? A nice Armenian girl. Not Maral. Maybe Sophie Agahigian. She's pretty."

Jack said, "Sure."

I knew Jack was lying. He'd marry some *odar* just to spite us. "Go to bed. And please use the stairs from now on. I don't want you to break your neck."

Things were okay for a few weeks. I noticed that Toros had stopped referring to Jack as Mr. Romance, Donkey, and Squash Head. For his part, Jack arrived on time to the market and attended church without complaint. But the boy got out of bed in the morning with dark circles around his eyes. I suspected he was still sneaking out after we were all asleep.

One night when we were lying in bed, Toros complained to me that money was disappearing from the cash box at the store. Just a few dollars here and there, but it had started to add up.

"Do you think it could be the boy?" he asked.

"Maybe," I answered. "Maybe you should start paying him."

"He gets an allowance," protested Toros. "We give him food and a bed. We buy his clothes. What more does he need?"

"His work is worth something, Toros. Maybe you should make him a partner in the store."

"His reward for stealing should be partnership?"

"Why would he steal from himself?"

"I'll think about it," Toros said.

"His birthday is next week," I reminded him.

"I said I'll think about it." He rolled over and went to sleep.

But I couldn't shut my eyes. As I lay in the dark, listening to the noises of the house, I heard the creak of the attic stairs and then the click of the front door as it closed. After pulling on a day dress and a pair of shoes, I watched from the back porch as Jack loped down Lincoln Street. I suspected he was heading for the market and decided to follow.

When I reached the foot of Lincoln Street, I crept into the alley behind the store, where the blue convertible was parked. Through the screen door I spied Jack and his buddies Danny Dedayan, Bobby Goulian, Joe Pellegrino, and Tim Flanagan sitting around a table in the back room. A rope of smoke curled around the bare lightbulb and spread into a cloud above their heads. The Italian slapped cards onto the tabletop, where quarters were stacked in small columns. Each of the other boys, including Jack, held a slim-necked brown bottle. I was thankful Vartanoush Chahasbanian rested in her grave, because I could imagine what she would have said about this scene.

I stood there for another moment, thinking that I hadn't seen Jack look so relaxed and happy in years. There was a time when he made silly puns as we worked in the garden. I now couldn't remember the last time he had told me a joke or even smiled at a family meal. Just then Jack, after laughing at something the Irish boy whispered in his ear, leaned back in his chair to drink his beer. Beer?

I yanked open the door. "Okay, boys, game's over."

Their eyes bugged out of their heads as if the Mother of God herself had appeared in their midst. Jack's face tightened into a grimace, and his shoulders bunched together. Only Danny Dedayan, that snake charmer, said, "Mrs. Chahasbanian. I haven't seen you in a long time. How's your health?"

"How's your mother's health, Danny? I haven't given her a call in months."

That shut him up. The Italian gathered up the cards, and the others shuffled to their feet.

"I think you might want to leave the quarters where they are," I said. "And pour out those bottles in the sink."

"Ma," Jack protested.

"We'll discuss this when we're alone," I warned him.

The boys mumbled good night and sped off in Danny Dedayan's car.

"Pull up a chair," I said to Jack. I carried the jar they had been using as an ashtray to the trash barrel and emptied it, then sat down myself.

"Have you been stealing money from the register?" I asked.

Jack hung his head. "We've been playing cards, and I've had some debts."

"Whose quarters are these?"

"The guys'! I didn't take them from Pa, I swear."

"Then give them back. Drinking, smoking, lying, stealing, gambling. Where are the dancing girls? Have I left anything out?"

He shrugged.

"Thou shalt not smoke cigarettes. Thou shalt not gamble. Thou shalt not steal from thy father's store. There are a few more commandments, but you can start with these."

"Okay," he said as if he meant it.

Jack locked the door, and we walked home in silence. Leaves shifted in the breeze, and a lemon moon hung over us. Bits of glass in the pavement sparkled under the streetlights. I looked at Jack, who had his hands shoved into his pockets and his chin almost resting on his chest. Poor thing, I thought. Teenagers were a terrible American invention.

For Jack's eighteenth birthday I baked a chocolate cake. Joy helped me roll, cut, and stuff dumplings for *mantabour*, which

Jack loved. Toros, without informing anyone, hired a man to paint new gold letters on the store's front window: T. Chahasbanian & Son. In the late afternoon, Joy, Toros, and I stood out front admiring the new sign when Jack drove up after a round of deliveries.

Jack parked the truck and joined us on the sidewalk. I watched a dozen competing emotions play across my son's face. I think pride was one of them, but it was jostled to the side by what looked like dread.

"Happy birthday, son!" Toros clapped Jack on the shoulder, and the boy winced.

"Thanks, Pa."

"What do you think?" Toros asked, gesturing at the window.

"I don't know what to say," the boy replied.

"Try 'Thank you,'" Joy suggested.

"Yeah. Thanks," said Jack.

They closed the market, and we went home for dinner. Jack kept running his fingers through his hair and glancing around nervously all through the meal. He wouldn't have noticed if the *manti* had been made out of rubber the way he bolted them down.

While Joy did the dishes and Toros snoozed on the couch, Jack headed out to water the garden. I trailed him as he dragged the hose toward the tomato plants.

"Do you have something to tell me, Jack?"

He sighed.

"You didn't like Chahasbanian and Son?" I asked.

"That's not it," he said.

"Then what?"

"I signed up."

"For what?" I asked.

"Today I went to the recruiting station and joined."

"Joined what?"

"The army, Ma," he answered.

I didn't know whether to slap him or start crying. "*Vay babum!* Are you out of your mind? Do you want to march around a strange country shooting at people who've never done you any harm and then come home in a box?" I sank into a lawn chair, shaking my head.

"I'd have been drafted eventually. They promised I'd go to Germany. There's no shooting in Germany, Ma."

I saw newspaper images of concentration camps. Walking skeletons, stacks of bodies, piles of hair. "They kill Jews there, Jack."

"The war is over, Ma. They're not killing Jews."

"That's because there are no more Jews to kill. Do you think they can tell the difference between an Armenian and a Jew?"

"Don't get yourself going, Ma."

I was adrift in a river of misery. "Moses has practically disowned us. And now you're going to get yourself shot and killed. Next year Joy will run off with a traveling salesman. Why did I have children? All they do is stab you in the heart."

"Don't talk crazy, Ma. I won't get shot working in the commissary. I'll be back. I promise."

"Have you told your father?"

"I kind of hoped you'd talk to him," he said.

"When do you leave?"

"Basic training starts in six weeks."

Toros took the news better than I did. He spewed out some plastic phrases about the boy getting some discipline, learning a thing or two, becoming a man, and so forth. I went through all the handkerchiefs in my drawer, while Jack and Joy took turns patting me on the back.

When Arsinee came over on Saturday to help me make *beoregs*, I related the whole sorry tale.

"Germans aren't Turks," she reassured me.

"The Turks taught the Germans what they know," I said.

"But Germany lost the war. They are on their knees apologizing."

"Tell that to the dead Jews."

"He's going to be fine, honey. The worst you have to fret about is that he might come home with a venereal disease."

"*Aman im!* This is how you comfort a friend?"

She laughed. "Can't you take a joke?"

"Some joke."

"Think of it this way," she said, trying to make me feel better. "The boy wants to see some of the world before settling in your small corner of it."

"You think he'll come back?"

"He'll be back, Zabelle."

"Look at what happened with Moses," I reminded her.

Arsinee said, "We both knew that boy wasn't coming back. And we both know this one will."

CHAPTER ELEVEN

The Wedding

(HENNIKER, NEW HAMPSHIRE, 1960)

Jack sent us postcards and photographs from all over Europe. My favorite was a picture of my uniformed son standing in front of a tulip bed with a blond-braided Dutch girl who wore a long skirt and wooden shoes. For Christmas the first year he was in Germany, he mailed me a wooden cuckoo clock, which we hung in the living room. I didn't wind the clock, because the sound of the bird got on my nerves, but it looked nice on the wall.

While Jack was away, Joy graduated high school and found work as a secretary at the Underwood Factory just up the street. A few weeks after she started her new job, a slim envelope with a California postmark dropped through the mail slot. On an engraved card I read that the Reverend and Mrs.

Thomas Aiken were pleased to announce the marriage of their daughter Sarah to the Reverend Moses Charles. I was stunned. I had bought a sky blue suit to wear at Sarah and Moses's wedding, assuming that the invitation would be on its way. How could you not invite your mother to your wedding?

Moses called minutes after I had opened the envelope, as though he had timed its arrival. The telephone receiver felt like a poisonous snake in my hand. Moses explained that he and Sarah had married in a small ceremony in the Aikens' living room, with only a handful of friends as witnesses.

"I didn't want you and Pa to have to come all the way out here just for that," he said.

What was I supposed to do? Sit in the mud beseeching God to put an end to my wretched existence? Rage at my firstborn son that he had broken my heart and would soon drive me into my grave? The tie between Moses Charles and the Chahasbanians had thinned to a spider's filament, which couldn't bear anything heavier than a dust mote.

I pretended Moses was my second cousin twice removed. I said, "Send us some pictures so we can see what you were wearing. When do we get to meet Sarah?"

"Next year," he promised, "we'll be out to see you."

I thought, I'm not going to start stuffing grape leaves for that visit until the plane lands.

As soon as I hung up the phone, I began to cry. I was red-eyed and limp as a rag when Joy and Toros came home after work.

"Zabelle," Toros said, "you can't make a donkey into a horse. Moses wanted it this way. The Aikens are a fine church family. They're not Armenian, but you can't have everything."

Joy said, "Don't worry, Ma. You can wear the suit to Jack's wedding."

In the old country, parents arranged marriages for their children, but you couldn't do that in a country where girls and boys mixed with each other like so many plums and apricots in a bowl. When Jack came back from the army, Toros trotted Armenian girls in and out of the house like show ponies. You'd think he would have learned his lesson.

Toros even went so far as to get the Hovanessians and their daughter Takouhie to drive up from Philadelphia for a weekend. Of course, just as the Hovanessians were pulling up in front of the house, Jack was pulling his car out of the back driveway. He didn't show up again until Monday, after the poor girl had been carted back to Pennsylvania.

Toros and Jack did come to a kind of peace at the market, though. While Jack was in Germany, Toros had hired a fellow named Hagop Marashlian, who had robbed him blind over the course of ten months. After firing Hagop, he took on Raffi Janjigian. Raffi, an easygoing and trustworthy boy, was a little short on brains. So after two years' absence, when Jack finally cranked down the market awning, his father gave silent thanks to God.

Chahasbanian and son didn't step on each other's toes. Toros kept the insults down, and the army had taught Jack how to pay attention to details. Not that Jack had completely reformed. When I did the laundry, I smelled cigarettes and perfume on his shirts, but at least at home he was on good behavior.

We never met any of his phantom girlfriends, until the time Jack invited Helen Foster to the house for dinner. For him to take such a step, I knew marriage had to be looming on the horizen. I was disappointed that she wasn't Armenian, but she was polite and modest, and her pocketbook matched her shoes. She worked as a receptionist for a dentist in Newton, where she shared an apartment with a few girls she had met in secretarial school. Toros questioned her and seemed satisfied when she said that she attended a Baptist church and owned a copy of the Bible.

After Jack and Helen announced their engagement, we were invited to pay a visit to Helen's family in New Hampshire. Her five sisters and five brothers, plus their spouses and children, gathered at the rickety old Foster farm. We drove up the rutted road and parked next to rusting pickup trucks and station wagons in a weed-filled yard. Toros, Joy, and I crossed planks over puddles to the house.

Helen, with Jack standing uneasily at her elbow, introduced us to the crowd, one by one. I despaired of ever being able to tell them apart. The brothers were thin and rangy with slack jaws, and the sisters were distinguishable only by the lengths and styles of their brown hair.

There were names and nicknames. Helen, who was the youngest, was called Princess; the eldest sister, Roberta, was called Bobo; the skinny Hubert answered to Fats. A sister with a streak of white through her black hair was called the Skunk. Her real name escaped me, and I couldn't imagine calling someone Skunk.

Helen's mother was long dead. Her father was a dried-up, mean-tempered old man who smoked three packs of cigarettes a day and lived on saltines and coffee. His beard and his fingers were stained yellow; he was practically toothless. His hearing was bad, so when I sat next to him on a ragged sofa, I had to shout, which gave me a headache.

Everything about the Fosters was loud. They all talked at once, so everyone yelled to be heard. There were dogs underfoot, barking and yapping. In the middle of our visit a raccoon wandered out from behind the refrigerator and scratched a four-year-old boy—one of Helen's nephews—who cursed like a sailor at his mother. I suddenly came to a deep understanding of the wisdom of arranged marriage. Not only was Jack marrying Helen, but the Chahasbanians were being joined to the Fosters, and it was not a union that I relished.

Toros was horrified, too, and we spent the drive home trying to convince Jack to give the girl up. I cried, then Toros yelled, then I pleaded and cried some more. Jack was as responsive as a store mannequin—his eyes were flat, and he seemed not to hear a word we were saying. In fact, I think our attempts to persuade him to call off the marriage only hardened his resolve.

On the eve of Jack's wedding, I turned in my bed like a rotisserie chicken.

Toros growled, "Woman, if you don't let me sleep, I'm going to be in a foul temper tomorrow." He rolled onto his side and added, "Get some sleep. It's in the Lord's hands."

I envisioned Jack and Helen in their wedding clothes, standing on God's outstretched palm. This thought calmed me, until a swarm of Fosters came running out of God's sleeves, and I felt terrible again.

"Dear Lord," I prayed, "please prevent this catastrophe. Please save us from the Fosters. Let Jack come to his senses and forget about Helen. . . ."

Poor Helen. I imagined the look on her face as Jack jilted her at the altar. I wasn't heartless. I knew that she loved him. If only the girl had been an orphan, there wouldn't have been all those wretched Fosters as part of the bargain. I knew about suffering at the hands of a mother-in-law, though. I didn't want to make life more difficult for Helen. She had probably barely survived her childhood among those people.

I rolled onto my side. There was nothing to be done now. At least Moses and Sarah wouldn't be present to witness our disgrace. At least the mother of the groom was allowed to cry.

The rectangle of sky outside the window was blue, and the air that moved the bedroom curtains was mild. I had hoped for rain. I zipped the back of Joy's dress and sighed.

"Ma," said Joy, "Helen's a nice enough girl. It could be worse. He could have married the one in pink stretch pants I saw him with on Mount Auburn Street."

I didn't say anything.

"Think about the kind of women he met when he was in the army," Joy added.

I didn't want to think about that. The Fosters were bad enough. "What about that family?"

"He's not marrying them." Joy went to the dresser and picked up the brush.

"Jack and Helen will be living downstairs, and the whole circus will come to visit." I sat heavily in the armchair. I rolled a stocking and wearily pulled it over my foot.

"You can have a headache," Joy said.

"A lifelong headache." I finished with the second stocking and bent to put on white pumps. "Where's your father?"

"He's in the living room."

"And Jack?" I stood and smoothed out my sky blue suit with white trim. It was a little tight in the waist. Too much ice cream.

"He went out with his friends last night, and stayed at Danny's."

"Up to no good." I had given up tracking Jack's comings and goings. He was a man, more or less, and he wasn't my problem anymore, he was Helen's.

Toros paused in the doorframe, tucking a white handkerchief in his suit pocket. "I'll be in the car. Don't keep me waiting long."

I jabbed my hatpin into place.

"It's a wonder you don't stab yourself." Joy, who stood behind me, a head taller, adjusted her own hat in the mirror.

"Don't forget your gloves." I picked up the white pocketbook and marched out of the room.

We stopped on Nichols Avenue for Arsinee. She was our sole ally. The wedding would be small. Helen insisted on paying for everything herself with the savings from her receptionist job. Only the immediate family and a few close friends were invited. Forty Fosters and a handful of Chahasbanians.

"Look at the three of you. Might as well be a hearse," Arsinee commented as she climbed into the backseat. She pinched the back of Joy's hand. "Let's hope they're happier on your wedding day."

"Don't start, Auntie," Joy said.

Arsinee continued. "You couldn't ask for better weather.

I'll bet Jack will knock them over in that white tuxedo. How long a drive is it? What kind of church do these people go to?"

I turned in my seat, annoyed by Arsinee's chatter, and snapped, "We've talked about it enough."

"I know why you're upset," Arsinee said, leaning forward. "They're devil worshipers, and you're going to be sacrificed on the altar, or better yet, you're on the menu. Some tasty Armenian stew. I'd better watch out myself, I'm the tastiest one of all."

Toros, who generally ignored Arsinee, shouted, "Enough, lest God strike you down."

Arsinee rolled her eyes and slumped back in the seat. She muttered under her breath, "No one could ever accuse the Chahasbanians of enjoying themselves."

An hour and a half later we rolled into the church parking lot and past a cluster of Foster men in suits who stood around the back of a faded green pickup truck. The Fosters were drinking from paper bags out of which poked long brown bottlenecks. Because our family didn't believe in liquor, no alcohol would be served at the reception, so the Foster boys were getting a jump start.

"Drunken fools," Toros muttered.

Arsinee commented, "At least they're not drinking in the church."

I looked at my watch: 10:45. In thirty minutes these degenerates would be our family.

* * *

As we entered the church vestibule, we walked into a cloud of coral taffeta dresses. The bridesmaids—several of the Foster sisters and two other girls who didn't resemble them—were passing through.

"Don't you look nice," said a fat Foster sister.

"Beautiful day for a wedding," said one with glasses.

"You come with us, doll," the Skunk said to Joy. "Wait until you see Helen's dress."

Joy cast a worried glance my way. Then she was caught up in the swarm moving toward the stairs. One of the Fosters called out behind her, "Jack's in the minister's study up front. I bet he's climbing the walls. Maybe his daddy could give him some advice." A ripple of laughter rose from the stairwell as they disappeared.

"A father's duty," Toros said grimly. He headed for the study.

Arsinee and I went into the coatroom, where we were alone.

Arsinee said, "I'd love to be a fly on the wall in that room."

"He's given up wasting his breath. A few Bible verses, that's all," I said.

"No advice about the birds and the bees?"

I shot her a cold look.

"What's your problem?" Arsinee asked. "You act like Jack's committing bank robbery and he's made you an accomplice. There's nothing the matter with that girl."

"What about her family? They're drunks, hussies, and probably criminals. He doesn't care about the shame he's bringing on us."

"Try to look at it from his point of view. Haven't you ever wanted something?"

"What do you mean?"

"Haven't you ever done something that might be against the Commandments, or cause a scandal, or make Toros angry?"

My mind flew like a homing pigeon to a night more than twenty years before when I had kissed a man who wasn't my husband. I hadn't thought about Moses in a long time. I wondered how he was. I knew that he and Big Nose finally had two children. Those kids must have graduated high school by now, I figured. About ten years ago he had sent me a note that said, "In dreams and in heaven, we shall meet." It was written in small, precise letters on a plain card. He hadn't signed it, but I knew it was from him. I put the card in the bottom of my sewing basket, and after awhile I threw it away. I had never told Arsinee, and I certainly wasn't going to confess now. Anyway, what did that have to do with Jack's marrying into a nest of thieves? "It says in the Scriptures, 'Be ye not unequally yoked.'"

Arsinee clucked in exasperation. "You've gotten as pigheaded as your husband."

It was true. That Bible verse popped out of me like Toros was a ventriloquist and I his dummy. I guess that's what years of living with someone can do to you.

* * *

In a long white dress that covered her neck to toe, Helen looked lovely walking down the aisle. I barely noticed the stooped old man walking by her side. I got a little teary seeing Jack so handsome in his white tuxedo. I remembered the time he had set the sewing machine on fire when he was four years old. The boy was always into mischief, but he had such a disarming smile. Now he was all grown up, though, and he hadn't turned into an arsonist, or a bank robber, or a gambler. He was a reliable partner in the family market.

Maybe it was the country church, or the calm tones of the white-haired minister, but by the end of the ceremony I was filled with love and compassion for everyone. After the service, I decided to find Helen downstairs to have a little heart-to-heart.

I floated down the stairs on a wave of warmth and understanding. I was a mother-in-law going to speak a few kind words to my new daughter-in-law. My new role made me think of Vartanoush, may she stay on her own side of the bridge of hair.

"Mrs. Chahasbanian," said Helen.

"Call me Mother," I pleaded, inspired by a sudden upswell of affection.

Helen blushed, and her eyes filled. "You don't know how much that means to me, Mother."

I patted the girl's hand. "You look so beautiful, dear. Don't cry."

There was a knock at the door. "Helen, are you in there?" asked Jack.

"Come in," said Helen.

I turned to Jack as he entered the room. "I wish you both happiness." As I left the room, I said to Jack in Armenian, "Sometimes I think God made you handsome to make up for the trouble you cause."

The reception was held at the VFW hall in the next town. We were seated at the head table with the wedding party. Danny Dedayan, Jack's best man, was sitting across from us with his *odar* wife, and he winked at me.

Arsinee whispered into my ear in Armenian, "This isn't so bad, is it?"

Then came the first toast. Fats Foster stood, swaying slightly, his suit hanging from his skinny frame. He said, "Well, now, we wish Princess well whether she deserves to wear white or not. And Jack, buddy, we don't know you that well, either, but we hope you're the man for the job." He slumped into his seat. People laughed, and someone yelled, "Hey, Fats, let's see what's on the other side of your tie."

Fats belched loudly and got to his feet. He lifted his tie so its underside was displayed in front of his face. There was a naked woman with enormous breasts painted onto it. This brought a round of laughter and applause.

I thought I was going to faint. I glanced at Toros, whose face was ashen. Joy blushed crimson. I couldn't bring myself to look at Helen and Jack. I stared at the wilting salad on my plate.

The rest of the toasts were mild by comparison, but I wasn't listening. I felt as though I were sitting on sharp stones. I eyed the clock like it was my enemy. Because there was no drinking and no dancing, people got bored and began to leave soon after the cake was served. Finally Joy, Arsinee, and I got up from the table. We kissed Helen and Jack good-bye and headed for the ladies' room. Toros started out to the car.

Joy and I stood outside the ladies' room, waiting for Arsinee. Bobo appeared from nowhere in front of us.

"I've been looking for you," she said, pointing a bony finger at me. Bobo's hat tilted off her head, and her dress was wrinkled.

Joy and I instinctively moved closer to each other. My heart started pumping faster.

Bobo narrowed her eyes and leaned down toward me. "I don't know who the hell you think you are sitting there looking like you're too good to wipe your own behind."

My eyes widened. I couldn't believe what I was hearing. I glanced around to see if other people were within earshot and felt relief when I saw we were alone. Then I realized I should be more nervous. What if Bobo had a gun in the purse she had slung over her arm like a dead animal? Joy placed her hand on my shoulder in a protective gesture.

"You think you're getting the booby prize, don't you, because Princess doesn't come from a fine family? Well, let me ask you, what kind of sack of shit are we getting? You people can't speak English right, you're dark skinned, and you're from Russia. No one can pronounce your name. For Princess's sake, I tried to convince Pa that Jack wasn't a Negro Communist, but you know what? I'm going to let him think what he wants. The only thing you people have going for you, as far as I can see, is that you're not Jews. And if I ever hear of you giving shit to Princess, there's going to be all hell to pay." With that, Bobo turned on her heel and stomped off.

It was as though someone had knocked the breath out of me. Jack, a Negro Communist? What could that possibly mean? I felt Joy shaking me.

Joy asked, "Ma, are you okay?"

I took a deep breath. "And on top of everything, there really is insanity in the family."

Arsinee joined us. "Is that woman drunk?"

"Now you see what I'm talking about," I said shakily. I felt off balance. It had never occurred to me that the Fosters might not want us in their family. I guess they thought of us as foreigners. We were immigrants and they were real Americans. But a sack of shit?

The Skunk appeared at my side, and I jumped. She patted my arm kindly and said, "You look like you could use some of this, Mrs. Chuzabunyon."

She thrust a glass of Coke into my hand and continued, "I'm really sorry about Bobo. Mom died when Princess was a baby, and Bobo had to take over. She doesn't mean half of what she says."

The Skunk seemed the kindest one in the Foster family. Besides, her hat was in place, and her dress was smooth. I said, "Thank you, Skunk."

Suddenly I felt thirsty, really thirsty. I gulped down the Coke, draining the glass in a flash. It was sweet, but there was an aftertaste of something like insect repellent.

Joy grabbed the glass from me, sniffed it, and asked Skunk suspiciously, "What did you put in here?"

The Skunk pulled a flask from the top of her dress. "Vodka. It's medicinal."

We didn't have cooking sherry in our house because Toros forbade it. At our church we used grape juice for communion. The only alcohol I had ever smelled was in the vanilla extract. Now a shot of vodka was in my stomach, and within minutes it rocketed through my blood. It felt like someone was undoing an invisible girdle inside my head.

Joy steered me toward the exit, with Arsinee next to me, laughing out of the side of her mouth. Skunk called after us, "It will do her good, I promise you."

They rushed me toward the car.

"What's the big hurry?" I asked. I felt very sleepy, like there was syrup in my veins. "I want to sit down." I slumped onto the parking lot blacktop.

"Ma, get up!" Joy pulled me to my feet and sped me across the last ten feet to the car.

"Joy, sit in the front seat with your father," Arsinee instructed as she pushed me into the backseat.

"What took you so long?" snapped Toros.

"We got into a little discussion with Bobo," said Arsinee.

"They think Jack is a Negro Communist." I wanted to cry. I wanted to hug Skunk. "They're our family now."

"Don't dwell on it," Toros said firmly, steering the car onto the road. "If I weren't a Christian, I might have taken that filthy tie and strangled Fatso with it. We should thank God we saved poor Helen."

"I told her to call me Mother," I said. "She lost her mother when she was a little girl. Me too." I saw all the motherless orphans in the world holding hands, stretched out along the toll road. Tears started rolling down my cheeks. "Toros drowned the mother mouse in a bucket with bleach, and all the babies, they were left to be eaten by the cat."

"What are you talking about?" Toros bellowed. We were on the highway, and he couldn't turn around. "Why are you sitting in the backseat?"

My sadness soured to anger. "Why are you shouting at me? Why don't you talk to me in that respectful tone you used with your mother? Why doesn't Moses talk to me like that? I treated him like he was the best part of me, and now he acts like he'd be happier if I didn't exist. We haven't seen him in two years. Did I do something wrong? All Jack says to me is hello, the weather is nice today, mind your own business. Now he's married into this family of drunks with naked women painted on their ties."

Joy said, "Ma, please calm down."

"My daughter loves me. I wish I had all daughters. Who needs a husband? I should have had more daughters."

"Zabelle, have you lost your mind? Joy, what did that Bobo woman say to your mother?"

Arsinee snorted.

"I am calm. I am perfectly calm, you just don't want to hear what I have to say. Too bad for you. My tongue is loose, and you're going to have to listen to it." I ripped off my hat, unbuttoned my jacket, and undid the hook at the side of my skirt, which was cutting into my waist. "I'll eat all the ice cream I want."

"What does ice cream have to do with anything?" shouted Toros.

"I told you not to shout." Weariness crept from my eyes, down my spine, to my toes in their pointed shoes. I kicked off the shoes. So Jack had married into a family that hated Communists, Negroes, Jews, and Armenians, and I was drunk. I shut my eyes, but I wasn't really asleep.

"She's asleep," said Arsinee.

"If I didn't know your mother, I'd suspect that she had been drinking," commented Toros.

Joy didn't respond.

Arsinee said, "It was a tough day."

Without opening my eyes, I said, "No one calls his own yogurt sour." And I went to sleep.

CHAPTER TWELVE

The Suitor

(WATERTOWN, 1963)

In the Armenian Brethren Church there were three kinds of women: mothers, aunties, and young women on the road to becoming one or the other. Aunties dressed in black or gray, wound their hair in neat buns, and lifted their quavering voices in song from the front pews of the church. Although a few widows sat among them, the true aunties were what they call old maids in this country.

When Joy's twenty-seventh birthday came and went, and she still didn't have a boyfriend, I realized she was standing at a fork in the road. It was funny that I hadn't thought of it before—twenty-seven was old to be unmarried in that day—but I had never stopped to look at Joy and consider her as an independent person. She was my daughter, and unlike my sons, she had never brought me any grief, except during the first two years of her life when she didn't let me sleep.

Ever since Joy was a small girl, she had been shy about talking in front of people outside the family. When we stood on the church steps after Sunday service, chatting with people, Joy stood behind me, observing silently. It was only later, when we were alone, that she had plenty of comments to make about what was said. Joy was even more uncomfortable around boys her age and curled up tight like a potato bug if a boy spoke to her. I started to notice, though, that when they weren't looking at her, she was studying the single men out of the sides of her eyes.

I brought up the subject with Arsinee, trying to figure out what to do, if anything.

"Maybe she doesn't want to get married. She likes her job at Underwood. You never know. Maybe she's happy the way she is," I suggested.

"Maybe, maybe not. It would be nicer for you if she never left. Someone to help with the housework and keep you company while your husband reads the newspaper."

"What do you think I can do to help her?"

Well, it turned out that the Melkonians, from our church, had just taken in their cousin, who was recently arrived from Beirut. The Melkonians lived on Nichols Avenue, a block down from Arsinee. As soon as she spotted Vartan Melkonian, Arsinee hatched a plot.

"Listen," she said, "it's not as though she has to marry him. Maybe she'll like him, maybe she won't. But wouldn't it be nice for her to at least get the chance to say no?"

People made a distinction between the aunties who had a choice and those whom fate had made too ugly or too peculiar to find a husband. I called Varsenic Melkonian the next day and invited them over for Sunday dinner.

The Melkonians were a dull couple—their hair was white, their skin and clothes were gray, and they both spoke in a sort of drone that could lull you to sleep if the room was warm and you had eaten a big meal. Sometimes Hagop Melkonian talked himself to sleep, breaking out with a whistling snore in midsentence. It had been a few years since we'd had them to our house, but they obligingly accepted my invitation and brought Vartan with them.

On first inspection he seemed to be in his right mind and of sound limb. He was short—his eyes were on the same level as Joy's nose—and his mustache drooped slightly at each corner of his mouth. His long nose flared at the sides, which made him look a little like a bull. He shook hands with Toros vigorously and beamed at me with a full smile, showing a small gap between his front teeth. He didn't appear to be more than five years older than my girl.

Joy stared at her plate, glancing at him through her lashes. This meant she was curious. I thought maybe she was impressed by his polite manner and the elegant Armenian he spoke. Joy spoke "kitchen Armenian," but during the meal she didn't say a word.

"What will you do for work?" Toros asked, pointing at Vartan with his fork.

The young man patted his mouth with a napkin. "I have arranged to work at my trade, as a tailor, in the shop of *Baron* Bilizekian. I start next week, Lord willing."

"Vartan has established a savings account so he can buy his own store," said Mrs. Melkonian.

"An ambitious young man," added Mr. Melkonian.

Vartan smiled. "First I must learn English. Also, I must find a place to live so I don't impose on my generous cousins."

"I'm sure some family will be happy to take you as a boarder. Maybe we can offer you a room," said Toros.

Joy's eyes darted toward me. I wasn't interested in Vartan as a boarder. I said, "The Kavjians might have a room. They're on School Street."

"We're in no rush to lose the company of our good cousin," Mr. Melkonian protested.

Joy and I went into the kitchen to make the coffee. I asked her, "Well, what do you think of him?"

"Who?" asked Joy.

She wasn't going to make it easy, that was sure. "Who do you think? Vartan!"

"What about him?" She tried to sound casual, but I could see she was blushing.

"He's not bad looking," I said.

"I don't want to talk about it."

"Arsinee told me Varsenic said he's in a hurry to find a wife."

"Ma, you and Arsinee mind your own business."

Letting the pantry door swing shut behind her, Joy went to the living room with the dessert tray. Two steps behind her, I decided I wouldn't give up so easily.

After eating three pieces of pakhlava, Vartan smiled at me with flared nostrils. "*Digin* Chahasbanian, this pastry is delicious, and your coffee is brewed to perfection."

Who wouldn't want a son-in-law who gave compliments like that? And he was Armenian.

Sometimes a word is like a seed. Drop it in fertile ground, and under the right conditions, a green shoot will appear, like a little miracle. Arsinee was sowing seeds over on Nichols Avenue, and I scattered a few of my own.

On Monday when Joy left her job at the Underwood Factory office, Vartan was waiting on the sidewalk. I don't know what he said to her, but I saw him bow to kiss her hand when they reached our front steps. I jumped back from the curtains before they saw me and ran to the back porch, where I sat on the couch like I had been roosting there for hours.

When Joy rounded the house, Jack was spraying the garden with the hose. Helen, who was due to have a baby in a few months, hung laundry on the line. Toros pestered a squirrel, whacking at the hedges with his cane. Without a word, Joy floated up the stairs and went to her room.

I know some mothers and daughters who tell each other every secret, but Joy and I weren't like that. I knew what she was feeling, not because she ever said it. I guess you might say that on occasion I could read her mind. But you didn't have to be a mind reader to know she was thinking about Vartan Melkonian.

Arsinee heard from Varsenic Melkonian that Vartan was seriously considering Joy as well. Varsenic said Vartan thought our daughter had beautiful eyes. He admired the care she took with her dress and the fact that she didn't wear jewelry or makeup. He wondered if she was as good a cook as her mother.

I told Arsinee to pass along to Varsenic the news that Joy could roast a chicken and that she had also sewn all the curtains in our living room. She was an excellent typist, and Mr. Parsons at the Underwood Factory office called her irreplaceable.

Arsinee laughed at me. "Are you going to send them a copy of her medical records?"

"Maybe just the dental records," I said. "She has perfect teeth. Not a cavity in her head."

"Who was that on the phone, Ma?" Joy asked.

"Arsinee."

"You've talked to her four times today."

"Only three." From her vantage point next door, Arsinee kept tabs on Vartan's movements. She also received frequent reports from Varsenic and called to keep me informed. Vartan had just left the house, heading our way, as expected.

"Ma, you and Arsinee aren't meddling, are you?"

"He knows a fine woman when he sees one."

"You're not answering my question."

"What should I have to do with it?" I said.

"You invited the Melkonians for dinner."

"They called me only that morning to ask if they could bring their cousin. For all I knew, he could have been a sixty-year-old one-legged knife grinder from Aleppo. It was your luck he turned out to be a bachelor with a gleam in his eye."

Joy groaned.

"Go put this on the coffee table." I handed her a bowl of candied fruit slices.

Toros, Joy, and I were lined up on the couch in front of *Perry Mason* when the front doorbell rang. Joy went to the door. Vartan presented her with a bunch of long-stemmed roses wrapped in florist's paper.

"I was passing through the neighborhood," he said, "and thought I would come to pay my regards to this lovely lady and her gracious parents." He beamed at me. There was something disarming about the gap between his teeth.

Toros gestured to an armchair. "Take a seat, sir."

We turned off the TV and sat there. Joy kept rearranging her skirt on the couch.

"So, Vartan, what do you think of America?" Toros asked.

"It's a fine country, sir. A very fine country. A proud land."

"You've hit on it," said Toros. "Pride. Pride will be this nation's downfall. But what's going on here is enough to bring down another Flood. You turn on the television, see half-naked women, drunk men, and insolent children."

Vartan nodded in agreement, furrowing his brow. "America's morals are not—"

Toros interrupted. "These are the signs of the last days, son. I read in Revelations"—here he thumped the Bible on the end table—"about the sinful deeds men will commit before the Second Coming, and then I read the same things in the newspaper. Christ's return is at hand." Toros stared into the air over Vartan's head, as if imagining Christ's arrival.

"You are right, *Baron* Chahasbanian. So right. It was only yesterday that I was telling my good cousins the very same thing," Vartan said.

There was a long silence. Toros's eyes were half-closed. I yawned and said, "I'm tired. We should go to bed, Toros, and leave the young people alone."

"I'm not tired," snapped Toros. He had no intention of leaving his daughter and the Beirut tailor alone.

"I've been reading the newspaper, and my English gets better each day," Vartan stated.

"That will help with your business," I said.

"How is business?" Joy asked.

"Not bad at all. Today alone, we received orders for three suits."

Toros's chin dropped to his chest. I elbowed him awake. Joy smoothed her skirt. Vartan had the good grace to make his farewell before Toros fell asleep again. Then Joy went to her room. As I lay in my bed, I imagined Joy in her bed, staring at the ceiling.

Everyone at church knew about Joy and Vartan. I heard the nasty gossip from the back of my head. Of course, one woman said, an old girl like her could only get a man fresh off the boat who didn't know any better. His attentions have something to do with citizenship, said another. But everyone smiled at the couple. The important thing was that Joy finally had a suitor.

When the annual Armenian picnic rolled around in August, the Melkonians, who didn't own a car, drove to Ararat Campgrounds with us. Joy sat between me and Toros in the front, with Vartan and his cousins in the back. We were practically family.

Jack and Helen arrived with Arsinee, whose children never attended Armenian functions. While Jack skewered cubes of beef for shish kebab, Helen, who was in the hazy final weeks of pregnancy, sat fanning herself in a lawn chair in the shade. Joy helped me spread a cloth over the picnic table and unpack the baskets of food. Arsinee chatted with the Melkonians. The sounds of the *oud* and *dumbeg* drifted to our table from the band's white tent.

We all crowded onto the benches for our lunch. Joy was pressed between Vartan and Toros, who gestured in agreement with each other about some theological point I hadn't cared to follow. Vartan would interrupt their discussion every now and again to pay tribute to various food items that crossed his plate.

After the meal, Vartan steered Joy toward the tent to watch the dancers. The rest of our group trailed after them, leaving me and Arsinee at the table.

"Vartan surely likes your cooking," she said.

"Any day now I'm expecting him to praise the taste of my tap water," I said.

"Almost too good to be true," she commented. "He seems to worship Joy. He and Toros are of one mind. If I hadn't seen him kick a dog on the street, I'd think he was perfect."

"A good husband?" I asked, assuming she was joking about the dog.

"Has he asked her?"

"Any day now," I said.

A week later, Arsinee and I sat on the back porch together as Joy and Vartan drove off in a borrowed car for an evening out.

Arsinee said, "If I were a wagering woman, I'd bet he's going to ask her tonight."

"Did you hear something?" I asked.

"Let's just say Varsenic Melkonian bought herself a new dress."

It hit me on the top of the head like an acorn out of a tree. Joy getting married? She knew nothing about managing a household. She knew even less about men. And what exactly did I know about Vartan Melkonian? He worked hard. He learned English quickly. He belonged to our church. But that was all we knew about him, and his cousins were so blind, they'd mistake a jackal for a lamb.

Vartan was at our table every evening, cleaning his smile with a wooden toothpick. How quickly he had insinuated himself into the heart of our family. And he hovered over Joy like a cat about to pounce on a sparrow. *Vay babum*, I thought, I might as well throw my daughter to the wolves.

After Arsinee had gone home and Toros went to bed, I sat in the living room, trying to read. I picked lint off my sweater. I stood at the window, watching for cars. Finally the white car stopped at our walk. Joy climbed out and marched up the front steps.

When she entered the living room I was in my chair, gazing at a missionary magazine.

"Hi, honey!" I said. "Did you have a nice time?"

She barely looked at me. "Yeah. See you in the morning, Ma." She hurried to the attic.

The next morning Joy and I were changing the sheets on the beds, as we did every Saturday. Of course, I was dying of curiosity, but I knew if I asked her anything, she'd snap shut like a clasp purse. So I looked at her from the sides of my eyes and held my tongue. She was like me—thoughts traveled across her face like banners in a parade. There went a happy thought, there went confusion, and then again fear. Finally she said something.

"Do you love Pa?" she blurted.

I smoothed the sheet and tucked it under the mattress on our bed. "I've lived with him for more than thirty years. He's my husband."

"That's not the same thing. Do you love him?"

I paused. Toros and I were part of each other. It was like asking the elbow if it loved the wrist.

Joy ran out of patience and said, "Vartan wants to ask Pa if we can get married."

I asked, "And what did you tell him?"

"I didn't give him an answer yet. He thinks I'm beautiful, Ma. He wants to take care of me and protect me. He said my life is a bolt of cloth ready to be made into a handsome dress by the right tailor."

"Very poetic," I said.

"What should I do, Ma?"

I had only a few seconds to plan my response. Was my sudden mistrust of him well founded? Maybe if she married him, the old country tyrant would emerge to make a misery of her life. Maybe she'd be happier staying with us. But on the other hand, this might be Joy's only chance for a husband and a family of her own. "You should do what makes you happy," I told her.

"I don't know what will make me happy."

Something about the bolt of cloth made me nervous. I couldn't ignore my misgivings. "I hear he has a bad temper," I said.

"Who have you been talking to?"

"Not just the kind that yells, but also throws things," I added darkly. "Arsinee saw him kick a dog." This didn't seem like enough evidence to convince Joy. My imagination took hold. "He might be the kind who keeps you locked in the house all week. Imagine that. Not even a walk to the store, just like those poor Moslem women."

Joy said, "Ma, you don't know what you're talking about."

"I also heard that they suspect he murdered a man for staring at his younger sister. They don't know for sure, because the man disappeared, and no one found his body."

"Who are 'they'? And why didn't you tell me this before?"

"I only just heard about it from Arsinee a few days ago. She got it out of Varsenic Melkonian, who had been sworn to secrecy by Vartan's mother."

Joy was stunned. "You should have told me right away. Were you so desperate to get rid of me that you'd let me marry a murderer? I don't even know if I can believe you." Her face knitted itself into a fury. "Tomorrow I'm going to tell him yes!" she shouted as she stormed out of the room with the basket of dirty sheets.

She wouldn't talk to me the rest of the day. I was a wreck. Even though I had made up that story about Vartan, I was convinced that it was true in spirit. Now my daughter was going to be married to that brute because Arsinee and I had been meddling.

Arsinee was furious at me. "Stop whispering," she yelled into the phone. "I can't understand anything you're saying."

"I don't want Joy to hear."

"This is what you wanted, isn't it?" she said.

"I don't know," I moaned. "I don't know what I want." My poor baby, I thought. What had I done?

During the church service Joy sat next to me as still as a stone. I could hear the blood rushing in her veins, though, and the sound of her heart thumping like it was in my own body. Vartan sat five rows ahead, and at the front of the church sat the aunties, their heads wobbling on their skinny necks. We all stood to sing the final hymn, and the hymnal trembled in Joy's hand.

After the doxology Joy fled down the stairs to the bathroom. I saw Vartan go after her, and I went to the top of the stairs myself, followed by Arsinee. I waited, but Arsinee went down to use the bathroom, or so she said.

Vartan bolted up the stairs like a stampeding bull, and I knew Joy had been saved. I overheard Joy and Arsinee on my way down.

"Auntie, I'm so glad you're here. My mother told me all about Vartan. I was afraid to tell him I didn't want to marry him for fear he'd kill me."

Arsinee said, "What did your mother tell you?"

"Everything you heard about Vartan murdering a man in Beirut."

Arsinee laughed. "I saw him kick a dog."

"That's all?"

"She gets carried away with her ideas sometimes. But you're better off without him."

"She made it up?"

Arsinee shrugged.

Joy saw me standing on the steps. "Ma, why did you tell me he was a murderer? Didn't you think I could make my own decision?"

I wasn't sure what to say. Joy's face was flushed, but she didn't seem angry. I joined them near the drinking fountain.

Joy said, "Leave me alone, the two of you. He wasn't for me. If you weren't such a busybody, Ma . . ."

"Me?" I asked.

Arsinee said, "Don't play innocent."

"Don't stick your nose in my business again, okay?" Joy glared at me.

I said, "It was Arsinee's idea."

"There she goes again," said Arsinee. "You know you started the whole thing."

"You're the one. . . . ," I protested.

"Enough," said Joy. "Pa's waiting." She headed up the stairs.

Arsinee turned to me. "So how did he kill that man in Beirut? With the pinking shears?"

"Don't gloat," I replied.

Joy stayed at home and kept working at Underwood. She was a fond aunt to Jack's daughters. Sometimes I worried that she missed having a husband and children. But we were right in getting rid of Vartan. A few months after Joy refused him, Vartan married Sophie Kazanjian. Over time, the women in our church realized he was the kind of man who bullied his wife in order to feel strong. When Vartan and Sophie came to church on Sunday, there was never a bruise showing—he was too smart for that. But we all suspected what her long sleeves hid.

CHAPTER THIRTEEN

The Survivor

(BOSTON, 1971)

On my dresser, among the snapshots of my grandchildren, I kept a framed photograph of Moses Charles—a black-and-white glossy his organization sent out to people who donated money. He wasn't just a church pastor anymore. He was also a radio preacher invited to speak at evangelical churches all over the country. He had launched his first northeast regional tour in New York City and would give a sermon at the Tremont Temple in Boston. Pastor Margossian had reserved seats for our congregation and had even chartered a bus.

I heard Toros beep the car horn in the drive. We were about to go to the airport to pick up Moses and his family. We hadn't seen them since their second son, Peter, was born. He wasn't a baby anymore, and Jonathan was almost fourteen. I sent both boys presents on their birthdays and received thank-you notes written in a beautiful looping hand by their mother and signed in their names. Sarah was the one who remembered my birthday and the one who had called to tell us they were coming to Boston.

"Ma!" Joy called up the stairs. "We're waiting." The door banged shut.

I opened the icebox again to admire the food. Joy, Helen, and my two granddaughters had helped me make stuffed grape leaves, *jajikh, dolma, kufteh,* and *lahmejun.* I had also prepared *ghadayif* and *pakhlava* and would have continued baking if Toros hadn't untied my apron and cast it into the laundry basket, saying, "Enough, woman."

Elizabeth, Jack's oldest girl, bolted up the stairs, breathless. "Grandma, the cars are running, and you'd better get out there before Grandpa has a heart attack."

Pausing on the landing, I smoothed my granddaughter's long hair and straightened the straps of her jumper. Elizabeth was eight years old, so my fussing didn't bother her. I rooted in my pocketbook for a hard candy, and when I couldn't find any, I slipped a quarter into her palm.

"*Shnorhagal em,*" she said, thanking me in Armenian.

"*Khelatsi aghchigs. Shad keghetsig es.* My smart and beautiful girl. I'll pay for you to go to Armenian school so you can talk with me."

The horn sounded from the street.

Why was I dragging my feet? I wanted to go to the airport, and I didn't want to go. The prospect of seeing Moses made me nervous. It's funny how that works—a baby who was closer to you than your own heart could grow into someone more intimidating than a stranger. But at least a stranger had no claim on you.

The whole family drove out to Logan Airport—me, Toros, Joy, Jack, his wife, Helen, their two girls. Arsinee had wanted to come, but even though we planned to take two cars, I told her there wasn't enough room. She had her own opinions about Moses, and I didn't need to hear any more from her.

We stood at the arrival gate, watching for Moses. I recognized his face in the sea of faces and felt a jolt of happiness. Next to him was Sarah, and behind her were the two boys. Jonathan was a skinny teenager, with a mouth full of braces. It was the first time I had seen Peter, except for some baby photos, and that boy looked more like me than my own children. In the center of his face was the nose of Moses Chahasbanian.

Moses Charles's eyes searched the crowd, passed right by us, and settled on some men to our left in suits, ties, and sunglasses. The men moved toward him, smiling, and I headed toward him as well, with the rest of the family behind.

Our three groups collided. Moses acted as though he hadn't expected us at the airport, and I guess we hadn't really discussed it when Sarah phoned. There was some confusion about where he was staying. Were these men taking him to a hotel? Was he coming home with us? His eyes went back and forth between his missionary men—these Bobby Lyle, Dick Baldwin, and Charlie Somethingtons with good haircuts—and us, his ragtag family, wearing King's Department Store all over us. I felt the embarrassment I could see on his face. I picked up Peter, my grandson, who studied me with serious eyes.

All that food was waiting at home. "Moses," I said, putting the boy down and taking his hand firmly, "we've made your favorite foods. *Manti, lahmejun, jajikh . . .*"

How could he say no to my good cooking? But I saw a stubbornness on his face that I knew only too well. I nudged Toros.

Toros said, "The attic bedrooms are ready, but maybe you'll stay someplace else?"

I held my breath.

Moses bowed his head and studied his clasped hands. "We'll go to Watertown," he answered.

Even though it was a weekday, we sat down to a Sunday dinner in celebration of Moses's arrival. Jack and Toros closed the store for a few hours. Joy inserted extra leaves in the dining-room table, setting out the good china and silver. I tied a clean apron around my waist and turned up the flame under the pilaf.

Moses's eyes darted around the room as though he were looking in the corners for a heavenly apparition. I heaped his plate with food and watched him move it from one side to the other.

"Ma, you didn't put enough salt in the *jajikh,*" Jack griped.

"It's fine the way it is," said Helen, coming to my defense. "What grade are you in now, Jonathan?" she asked.

"Eighth," he answered.

Toros said to Sarah, "Those Garabedian kids come in after school, and they'd run out with their pockets stuffed with candy if I didn't stand by the door with a broom."

"I don't know about that," Jack said.

"Elizabeth and Julie, if you don't stop right now, there will be no TV tonight, and I mean it," Helen admonished.

"She kicked me first," complained Elizabeth.

Peter, who sat next to me, tugged at my sleeve. "Can I have some more of those, Grandma?" He pointed at the stuffed grape leaves.

"We call them cigars," Julie confided.

"Moses, how many people does the Tremont Temple hold?" asked Toros.

"Two thousand," Moses said. He drummed his fingers again.

"Can you believe that my son, the little Armenian boy in knickers, has become a famous preacher speaking before two thousand people?" asked Toros.

After lunch Moses and Sarah went to the attic for a nap. Toros dragged Jonathan with him to the market, while Joy headed to her office. Helen offered to take Peter with her and the girls to the public library, but he wanted to stay home with me. Sitting on the couch with my grandson's head in my lap, I told him a story about a talking fish until he drifted into sleep. I slipped Peter's head to a cushion and covered him with a blanket. The house was still.

I heard the mail thud through the slot and scatter onto the floor of the front hall. I padded down the front stairs in my slippers, stooped over, and picked up the pieces of mail one by one. Amid the bills and a postcard for Joy was a plain white envelope addressed to me. There was no return address, and I didn't recognize the handwriting, but it was postmarked Worcester. Moses Bodjakanian, I thought. I wondered what he could want to say to me after all these years. Maybe the goddess of beauty had died, and he was looking to give me the ring. I tore open the envelope. Across the top of the white sheet, a note was printed in English.

"Dear Mrs. Chahasbanian, My father died last month. He asked me to send this letter to you. Sincerely, Zaven K. Bodjakanian."

I sat heavily on the bottom step and read on.

Dear Zabelle,

After my first heart attack, I decided to write you a letter, which my son Zaven has promised to send to you after I die. He doesn't read Armenian, so don't worry.

Some years ago, I sent you an unsigned note, which said, "In dreams and in heaven, we shall meet." Maybe that is the best way. We had our moment of happiness, and we each had a secret that no one could touch.

May God protect and keep you. Heaven is ahead.

Your Moses

Memories flashed by like a deck of playing cards being shuffled, then slapped onto a tabletop. I was a girl, sewing buttons on dozens of shirts, shining in the light of a boy's eyes. His shadow fell over my shoulder. A silver thimble lay like a promise in my palm. I was a young mother, bending over my son in the garden, who held up a zinnia he had just plucked from its stem. I stood in the dark hallway, staring into the room where my babies slept. Where had they disappeared to, the ones I loved? I saw the desert and the lost faces of my family. I remembered my first night in the orphanage after Arsinee left— I was lying in a strange bed, feeling smaller and more alone than a speck of dust.

Suddenly a small hand was on my shoulder. It was Peter. I hadn't heard him come down the stairs.

"Grandma," he asked, "why are you crying?"

I answered in Armenian, "Loneliness."

"What?"

I continued in Armenian, "My heart is a broken bowl."

"Say it in English, Grandma."

I heard the worry in his voice. I wiped my face with my apron and retrieved the letter from the floor. "A friend of Grandma's died, sweetie, and she's very sad."

He slipped his hand into mine. As we climbed the stairs, I heard voices beyond the living-room door.

"I don't know how to talk to these people," Moses said.

"Honey, they're your parents. Tell them about your work. Talk about the weather."

It was obvious they thought they were alone in the house. I should have opened the door and interrupted them. But wanting to hear what Moses had to say about me made me forget the little boy at my side.

"We have nothing in common," Moses continued. "We live on different planets."

"I know, hon," she said.

"And Peter's getting on my nerves, following my mother around like a puppy."

"She's his grandmother, dear."

"Don't I know it. He has that same hangdog look in his eyes."

We had heard more than we needed. Peter's face was full of sorrow. I whispered in his ear, "Let's get an ice cream at Grandpa's store."

We retraced our steps quietly and sneaked out the front door. As we walked down Walnut Street, Peter scuffed his sneakers along the sidewalk. My grandson was a cuckoo in a robin's nest.

"My daddy doesn't like me," he said.

"Yes, he does," I reassured him. "He's just a little grumpy today."

"Mommy loves me. And you love me. Right?"

I crouched to hug him. He rested his head on my shoulder, and I smoothed his hair. "I love you, *yavrum*. You are my very own boy."

At dinner Moses lectured us about his mission. His hair was blonder than I remembered it, and I felt pity for his vanity. I noticed how uncomfortable he was at our table and how he boomed at us as though we were an audience.

"When we were in Topeka, over four hundred people answered the call," he said.

I went to the kitchen for the dessert and coffee. Moses's voice sounded like the neighbor's lawn mower. Coming back with the tray, I paused in the doorway and surveyed the family gathered at the table.

Toros wasn't eating much. There were dark circles around his eyes, but they were bright with the excitement of having Moses in his home. Jack had finished his meal and was spinning a quarter on the tabletop. What he wanted more than anything was a cigarette, his secret vice I knew all about. Helen observed Jack quietly, watching his bad mood approach. Joy picked crumbs from the tablecloth.

In the living room, Elizabeth and Julie were lying on the floor, watching cartoons. Jonathan sat in my armchair, reading *Pilgrim's Progress,* and Peter slept on the couch, curled up like a puppy.

Moses rambled on, his words gathering like clouds near the ceiling. Pretty soon they'd be taking up all the space, and everyone would be forced under the dining-room table. That's where I wanted to be. Under the table, like a grain of rice that had fallen to the carpet. But you can't do that when there are stacks of dishes in the sink.

Over the next few days a black sedan came and went with Moses and his suit-wearing men. They were planning the Friday night meeting and visiting other ministers in the area. I took telephone messages like a hotel desk clerk.

Peter and I became great friends. He played "button, button, who's got the button" with me and his cousins. He helped me make pickles and punched down the *cheoreg* dough. He even picked up a few words of Armenian, which gave Moses a headache, I could tell. But I had decided to ignore my son and not notice that he was avoiding me. What can you do? They spend a small time in your body, a small time in your arms, and a lifetime walking away.

And I mourned Moses Bodjakanian. It had been dozens

of years since I had seen him. He wasn't a part of my daily life, but there was a small room that I visited once in awhile in the house of memory where he remained. Now that I knew he was gone from the world, it was as if someone had plucked a lucky stone from my pocket.

Suddenly Peter was at my elbow, looking like a dark-haired version of his father as a child.

I took his hand and said, "Let's go to the store and ask Uncle Jack for a candy bar."

I wish now that I had paid more attention to Toros during those days. Later Helen told me she found him sitting on Gigante's steps, muttering to himself in Armenian. She tried to talk with him, but he closed his eyes and shook his head. The night before Moses's big meeting, Toros told me a story I had never heard before.

We were lying in our bed, and the words poured out of his mouth like ashes. "I was in the store with my father when we heard shouts in the street. My father went out to see what was happening. The Turks were dragging away our neighbor, Vasken Hamparian. My father asked them what they were doing. They cursed at him, and one of them smashed my father on the head with a club and he fell in the street. His blood ran over the stones. I watched the whole thing, and did nothing. God will never forgive me."

That was how it was with us. We never spoke about those

times, but they were like rotting animals behind the walls of our house. He knew nothing about my experience in the desert, and that was the first I had heard of what he had known in Adana.

I said, "God has forgiven you, Toros." And we went to sleep.

The next evening a sleek gray limousine came to collect Moses. My son was a general in the Lord's army, and he went to prepare himself for battle.

Peter and I waited in the yard for everyone else to come down. We lifted the marble stepping-stones on the lawn to examine the bugs living underneath. Then we sat on the picnic bench and counted the pears in the tree in Armenian.

"Grandma, what's your last name?" he asked me.

"Chahasbanian."

"How come Daddy doesn't have that name?"

What do you tell a child? Because it's hard to pronounce? I said, "Nobody can be famous with a name like that."

"Why not?"

"You spend so much time spelling it for people, you can't get your work done."

"Can you write it down for me?" he asked.

I pulled a pen and an old envelope from my pocketbook and slowly printed the English letters.

He said, "When I grow up, I want to be a Chahasbanian."

I squeezed his hand. "When you grow up, you can be anything you want, honey."

One of Moses's men met us in the lobby of the Tremont Temple. We weren't with our church but had special seats in the first balcony, with a clear view of the stage. There were hundreds and hundreds of people, their bright faces all turned toward my son. The buzzing voices hushed when he stood behind the pulpit, and when he waved, they all clapped. He stood up there, gleaming under the lights, talking about water and Christ and righteousness. Moses's men were handing out paper cups of water, with a Bible verse inscribed on it. John 4:13–14.

Jesus answered and said unto her, Whosoever drinketh this water shall thirst again: But whosoever drinketh of the water that I shall give him shall be in him a well of water springing up into everlasting life.

When Moses had droned on at our house, stiff with discomfort, I had forgotten how charismatic he could be. Always an intense and introspective child, as an adult, he had reversed his coat, turning the internal fire outward. He radiated light. And when he spoke, it was as though he were appealing directly to you—not to the person to the right or left of you, or anyone else. He was as personal and loving as Christ himself.

Just before the intermission, Toros grabbed my arm. I don't know if it was the heat, or the excitement, or if he was still thinking about the story he had told me the night before.

He was sitting next to me, listening to his son, his heart thumping along, and then it sputtered and stalled.

It was awful to see the way his mouth worked the air. He turned gray. I didn't know what to do. Part of me was calm and alert, watching the events occur around me. But another part screamed and pulled at my hair. When I noticed Peter sitting gape mouthed beside me, I threw my sweater over his head.

Jack ran up and down the aisle, shouting for help. Helen loosened Toros's tie and unbuttoned his shirt. Elizabeth and Julie started crying. Sarah and Jonathan chased an usher, who called for a doctor. An ambulance was waiting outside for this kind of emergency.

I climbed into the back of the ambulance and held my husband's cold hand. His face was the color of cement, and he was trying to talk to me.

"What is it, Toros?" I leaned close to him.

"Don't feel bad. God has forgiven me. I'm going home." Toros closed his eyes.

I saw him as a young man on a white stallion, galloping through the streets of Adana. With a mighty sword he struck down the Turkish soldiers who approached his father, pulling the old man into the saddle behind him. The horse sprouted enormous wings and flew toward heaven.

I wanted to tell the ambulance driver there was no hurry. The spirit had gone out of my husband's body. I held his hand

and shut my eyes. The breath was going in and out of me, my heart plodding along like a workhorse. It was strange how someone you loved could die in front of you, and you kept on. You found food and put it in your mouth. You drank water. You walked, you opened your lips and words came out. Put on your clothes. Take off your clothes. Sleep. Dream. Survive.

The funeral was two days later. Moses gave the eulogy, which was eloquent and hollow, as though he were speaking of someone he barely knew. And then he was gone. I wish there had been a moment for us to talk before he left for Chicago. What would we have said to each other? I felt like I was wrapped in waxed paper, and everyone seemed far away.

I kept expecting to hear Toros yell from the other room, "Zabelle, come in here!" Then I saw his creased work shoes bowed on the floor of our closet, and I couldn't stop crying. Joy and Helen sent me out of the room, packed everything up, and put it in the attic.

Arsinee came to keep me company. We sat on the back porch under the shade of the grape leaves. For a long time we didn't speak.

I was thinking about Toros pouring coffee into my cup in the morning. And the way he read things out loud from the newspaper to prove the rotten state of the world. How would I sleep without his snoring?

"So, here we are," Arsinee finally said. She patted my hand.

"Yes," I said. "Here we are."

"When you get to heaven," Arsinee asked, "are you going to live with Toros?"

"That depends on where his mother's staying."

We laughed. And then we went to the garden to pull some weeds.

EPILOGUE

Hadjintsi Badmoutioune

(HADJIN, 1909)

There was, there was not, there was a girl named Lucine Kodjababian who lived in the town of Hadjin, Cilicia, in the Ottoman empire. In the same town, not very far away, lived a boy named Garabed Boyajian. One day Garabed and Lucine— who had never seen or at least never noticed each other in their respective seventeen and fifteen years—passed each other in the street and exchanged glances, which left each dreaming of the other.

Now, in our times, this isn't such a problem: a boy sees a girl, he wants the girl, he chases after the girl, he marries her, and sometimes the other way around. But in 1909 in Cilicia, when Garabed stared after the lovely Lucine, her face as radiant as her name implied, it was not usual that boys chose their wives, or that girls gazed back at boys in the street.

As a matter of fact, Lucine's cousin, with whom she was going to market to buy vegetables for the evening meal, said to the girl, "What, have you no shame?" So Lucine, who had been turning to look at Garabed, who was turning back to look at her as they walked with their companions in opposite directions, faced ahead, her cheeks burning.

Garabed himself was thinking, Who was that girl? He noted the dark, sleek hair that hung down the center of her back in a long braid twined with ribbon, and the small waist under her embroidered apron. He saw a hint of her shift's hem appear from under the overdress, and the cuff of her pants covering her slim ankles. In his memory her eyes burned like dark moons in the night-white sky of her face.

And what did Lucine remember? Not his handsome face with its proud dark brow or his head of thick, black hair. Not the plain of his shoulders that rose out of the sleeveless vest. Not the red sash tied where his baggy pants met his shirt, above the narrow hips. She remembered the way his fierce eyes locked on hers, making her want something.

Now Hadjin, a town perched on the Toros Mountains of Cilicia, had over forty thousand inhabitants, almost all of them Armenian. About the time that Garabed saw Lucine, news of massacres in Adana reached the ears of the Hadjintsis, who thanked God for the good fortune of their own safety, not realizing that this news was only a thin shadow of what was to come.

In Hadjin, the streets, which were straight and narrow, with houses on each side, rose into the hills, so that some rooftops were level with the next street. Thousands of *ojakhs* sent smoke from daily meals coiling into the air above. How would Garabed ever find out this girl's name? Would Lucine ever see this boy again?

For days, when they went into the street—to church, to the market, or on other errands—the boy and the girl searched for each other. Garabed tossed and turned on his *doshag* in his family's house and dragged his tired body through his daily work in his father's shop. A little over a mile away, Lucine, asleep in her family's house, dreamed of eyes that reached out to her like burning hands. The daylight alarmed her. She yawned and rubbed her eyes, ate less than usual, spilled pails of water, and tripped over invisible obstacles, to the point that her mother was sure someone had given Lucine the evil eye. Her mother insisted that Lucine wear a blue ribbon in her hair and hung a horseshoe set with blue stones over the door.

Finally, after several weeks of despair, Lucine, who was returning home from the baths with her cousins and her younger sister, saw the boy with the coal black eyes, carrying a large package over his shoulder, walking toward them. She was terrified that he would pass without noticing her, but just as their paths crossed, he glanced up and met Lucine's eyes. She felt a shock, as though someone had rapped on her head with a thimble, and then a dizziness. Garabed stopped stock still, his pulse pounding in his neck, considering briefly what to do, then dropped his package and ran after her as she turned a corner with the other girls.

"What's your name?" he called.

She paused for a second and then said, "Kodjababian. Lucine."

Her older cousin hissed at her, "Are you crazy? Why are you listening to that rude boy? Why are you shouting your name shamelessly in the street?" The cousin grabbed Lucine's arm and hustled her along.

Garabed went back to his package, a delivery his father had entrusted to him, and continued on his way, singing to himself. "I have found the girl, her name is Lucine, Lucine the light of my eyes, Lucine the light of the night skies . . ."

Garabed made a number of inquiries in the afternoon and found out the address of the Kodjababians, the family of Lucine, happy it was so close to his own neighborhood. In the next days he went out of his way while on errands to walk up and down the Kodjababians' street. But not once did he see Lucine, and the sight of the blank wooden door of her house only made his misery grow.

His father, who noticed with annoyance this increasing absentmindedness and the dark moons under his son's eyes, finally called the boy aside one afternoon. "Son," he asked, "what devil is it that plagues you? You act more and more like a ghost."

Garabed admitted to his father his love for this girl, Lucine, and begged the elder Boyajian to plead his son's case with the Kodjababians. Berj Boyajian, who had his eye on another girl for his son, wasn't happy—what was the world coming to when a boy thought he could choose his own bride?—but he regarded himself as a modern man, and he loved his son, so he decided to consider the boy's request. As with all such dealings, the process had to be handled carefully and with discretion, so as not to shame either family.

That evening Berj Boyajian consulted with his brother Sahak and the godfather of Garabed, Hagop Asadourian, both of whom agreed to make inquiries into the character of the Kodjababians before undertaking to contact them about the Boyajian family's interest in the girl.

Meanwhile, still suspecting that her listless daughter was under the cast of an evil eye, Aghavni Kodjababian called in *Digin* Isgouhi, the local healer, to put salt on her daughter's forehead and in her mouth. *Digin* Isgouhi, an old woman renowned for her cures, prayed over Lucine, scattering salt in the corners of the house as well as just outside the door.

"Don't worry, honey," the old woman reassured Aghavni. "This happens to a lot of girls at this age."

Lucine, who didn't want to admit that she was actually under the spell of a pair of eyes, tried to be more careful in order to assuage her mother's fears. But since the second time she had seen the boy—whose name she still didn't know—her dreams were filled with signs and portents she couldn't interpret and that she was afraid to share with anyone. What did it mean to dream of sitting down to a meal with strangers? What was the significance of chasing a white dove up a hill?

Garabed's godfather, Hagop Asadourian, found out that the Kodjababians were a respectable, although by no means wealthy, family, Lucine's father being a tailor and her uncle, who lived in a house connected to Lucine's, a smith. Lucine, Asadourian learned, had the qualities one would desire in the possible future wife of one's godson: she was chaste, modest, and obedient. She was not promised to anyone and was also the elder of two sisters, which meant there was no obstacle in approaching the family.

Digin Isgouhi, the healer who had cured Lucine of the evil eye, was enlisted by the Boyajians as an emissary. Stopping by Lucine's father's shop, she said to Missak Kodjababian, "The Boyajians are interested in Lucine for their boy, Garabed. It's a good family of merchants, and the boy has straight legs and a strong back. You couldn't find a better husband for Lucine: he's healthy, will inherit his father's business, and attends church. When can you serve them coffee?"

So it was that Hagop Asadourian and Sahak Boyajian appeared on Sunday afternoon at the Kodjababian household for coffee. Lucine's family had in the meantime made their own inquiries about Garabed and, deciding he was a worthy candidate, made the coffee sweet as a signal to their guests that they were favorably disposed toward the offer.

Of course, Garabed paced back and forth in the courtyard behind his house that afternoon, tugging impatiently at his hair. And Lucine, who didn't yet know the family negotiating for her was that of the boy with the coal black eyes, wondered who her future husband might be. Would he be ugly? Would he be kind? She brought a tray of coffee to the men who sat on cushions around a low table and kept her eyes cast down as the visitors glanced at her and then each other. Lucine demurely retired to the back courtyard of her house, where she twisted the end of her braid and felt her stomach churn enough to make butter.

The next week Garabed's mother, aunt, sisters, and girl cousins arranged to go to the same Turkish baths as the Kodjababian women. In the steamy clamor of the bath, the Boyajian women inspected Lucine from a distance: her limbs were straight, all the body parts were in their accustomed places as far as they could see, and aside from a few moles, her skin was unblemished.

Garabed longed to see Lucine again. The complicated process of negotiating a betrothal could take several months, and while, at this point, success seemed likely, he thought of the girl through the day and the night. Occasionally his mind would be diverted by something else—a conversation with a friend, an urgent errand for his father—but then Lucine would come back to him. It was the simultaneity of her presence and her absence that caused him pain.

So, enlisting the aid of one of the Kodjababians' neighbors, a boy about his own age whose sister was a friend of Lucine's, he passed her a note: "I beg you please to try to meet me tomorrow at the market in the afternoon. I'll be by the halvah seller. Signed, Garabed Boyajian."

Lucine was terribly upset by the note. It was improper for her to have a secret meeting with a boy, even her future husband. In any case, she couldn't go to the market alone and arranged for Mariam, her friend and neighbor, to accompany her on the pretense of buying some cloth.

Garabed stood waiting at the halvah seller most of the afternoon, his eyes searching the passing crowds for Lucine. The muscles in his legs ached from being tensed and released, and his ears were ringing when, finally, she and Mariam appeared. When Lucine saw Garabed and recognized him as the boy whose gaze had filled her with longing, she felt blood rush to her face. Garabed, suddenly struck dumb with fear himself, bowed to the girls as they approached. Mariam glanced at one and then the other and moved off a few feet, out of hearing.

Garabed said, "My family is speaking with your family."

"Yes," said Lucine. She cast her eyes down.

"It may be that we are to be married," he added.

"This is your doing?" she asked.

"Are you displeased?" he asked. It had occurred to him before that she might not share his feelings, but as he was faced with her now, this possibility cut through him like a sword.

"No. I am not displeased," she said, adding quickly, "Our families know better than we do about these things."

Mariam tugged at Lucine's sleeve; she said good-bye to Garabed, not daring again to meet his eyes, and the two girls hurried off.

Lucine lay awake that night, seeing above her in the dark a long, narrow face with wide, dark eyes that spat light. And

Garabed stared out the window at the moon, its light falling in on his bed, seeing in its features those of his future wife.

So, reader, the betrothal was accomplished in its time, and Garabed's family placed a ring on Lucine's right hand, which a year later Garabed himself placed on her left hand in a service blessed by God. Here it is customary to say that they lived happily ever after, but while they loved each other, and two children, Zabelle and Krikor, came of their love, long life and happiness were not their destiny. Garabed was part of a row of men who were shot by Turkish soldiers on the outskirts of Hadjin, and Lucine, after the demise of her infant son, died of exhaustion and hunger in a desert tent. Zabelle, whose story this is, lived to remember and forget the tale.

Glossary of Armenian, Turkish, and Arabic Words

Aghchig, mayr, hayr unis?	little girl, do you have a mother or father?
aghchigs	my girl
Aman im	Mercy me
basterma	cured, spied beef
Bitdi, getdi	done and gone
beoregs	savory filled pastry
Cheh	no
cheoregs	sweet, yeasted rolls
Der Hayr	Father (to address priest)
dev	devil, monster
djinns	demons
dolma	stuffed vegetable
doshag	soft, rolled-up mattress
Eh leh lepeleh . . .	Turkish children's song
Esh	donkey, ass
gadu	cat
ghadayif	pastry of shredded wheat, honey, and nuts
ghurabia	butter cookie
Hadjintsi Badmoutiuone	a tale of Hadjin

hammam	Turkish bath
Hanum	Mistress
jajikh	cold yogurt-cucumber soup
jarbig	clever, resourceful
Khelatsi aghchigs	my beautiful girl
Khent ek?	Are you crazy? (plural)
Khent es?	Are you crazy? (singular)
kufteh	Armenian meatball
lahmejun	Armenian pizza with ground beef or lamb
mantabour	dumpling soup
manti	dumpling
Mayrig	Mom
odar	non-Armenian
pakhlava	pastry of filo dough, honey and nuts
poghokagans	Protestants
saj	griddle
Shad keghetsig es	You are very beautiful
Shnorhagal em	Thank you
tahn	yogurt and water beverage
Vay	alas, oh
Vay babum	oh my father (idiom)
Voch	No
yavrum	sweetie, my darling
Yes hay em	I am Armenian

Acknowledgments

Thanks to Leo Hamalian, editor of *ARARAT Quarterly* in which "Armenian Eyes" and "The Balcony" first appeared, and to the Corporation of Yaddo for a quiet month. Gratitude to those who read and offered comments: Merloyd Lawrence, Paula Sharp, Susan Kricorian, Anne Carey, Tanja Graf, Maria Massie, Kim Witherspoon, Sally Wofford-Girand, Marlene Adelstein, Lola Koundakjian, and Elisabeth Schmitz. Thanks to Irene and Ed Kricorian, for answering my questions, and to James Schamus, my most critical and devoted reader. Mrs. Alice Kharibian told me her story and what she knew of my grandmother's. Mrs. Rachel Gayzagian's voice was in my head as I wrote.